THE UNEX...
Ghost stories from Malta and beyond .....

Vanessa Macdonald
2001

Printed and Published
by
Progress Press Co. Ltd.,
Valletta, Malta 2001
(A member of the Allied Group)

Reprinted 2002
2nd Reprint 2002

© Venessa Macdonald 2001 - 2002

ISBN 99909-3-063-5

DEDICATION

To my husband Ian, and my children
Kelly and Craig

ABOUT THE AUTHOR

Vanessa Macdonald was born and bred in Malta but then travelled extensively for 13 years before settling in Malta with her husband and two children. She has worked in journalism since 1993, waiting for the right time to indulge her passion for sailing and travel.

FOREWORD

There are so many books of ghost stories. Why another? One of the problems with the books I have read was that the stories had been handed down from generation to generation. Many had become legend, but what was the truth? How embellished had the stories become over the years? Let me give you an example.

There is a story about a house in Valletta. There are at least five versions of the story in circulation, all varying in some small but crucial detail. Which, if any, is the real version?

This is why I wanted to catalogue these first-hand accounts, all told to me by the person who had been involved (except for one story sent to me by mail which was so fascinating that I included it…). Most of the people I interviewed for this series, which had first appeared between 1994 and 1997 in The Weekender supplement of *The Times* of Malta, were people I knew or that I was referred to by mutual friends. All of them had told their stories before, some of them only to a handful of relatives.

I spent many afternoons in someone's living room or office, the person telling me the story jumping up to demonstrate a point, or shivering as they recalled some unpleasant detail.

Every single one of these people believed the story they told me.

Did I believe them?

Ghost stories have fascinated every generation, but one of the reasons we enjoy reading them is because we are not forced to believe them. Unless you have experienced one of these phenomena yourself, you will all too likely allow your scepticism to get the better of you. After all, if you believed… well, where could your imagination take you then?

We find it far more comfortable to write off the people who see ghosts as having hallucinated, as being emotionally distraught at the time, on drugs, having too vivid an imagination.

But if you have been through an experience which just cannot be explained, as I have, what then?

I know the people and the places involved in these stories. I did not set out to try to prove these stories scientifically, or to create a piece of research. These are stories of events which have shaped the lives of those who experienced them.

Believe them if you dare.

Most of the people interviewed are still alive, and the houses and places they refer to still stand. Some are now lived in by people who may be totally unaware of their past. This is why the names have been changed, except where indicated.

Vanessa Macdonald, 2000

CONTENTS

CHAPTER ONE

Say the word "ghost" and most people think of poltergeists, of bleak haunted houses with decayed shutters and overgrown gardens. Think again. These stories are about benevolent ghosts, who come back to see the living with a reassuring message, perhaps unwilling to cut themselves off from loved ones for eternity.

Others are about ghosts who may just have saved lives, sending messages to alert people to danger.

A Helping Hand

It was just a regular family gathering. Paul and Kate sat watching their son, Daniel, as Paul's dad fiddled with a few adjustments on his new video camera.

"OK, OK, it's working now," he said, while his wife bustled around in her usual way.

They had had lunch and were now sitting down waiting for something worth watching to come on to the television. But for the moment, they could think of nothing more enjoyable than watching Daniel learn how to walk.

He was just a year old and his steps as he made his way along the furniture still had the lurching, unbalanced quality of a tipsy sailor. He pulled himself up against his mother's skirt, then spied a toy on the other side of the rug and, without stopping to think of the consequences, he lunged for it. He was perhaps even more surprised than the onlookers to find that his foot had actually taken a step.

Kate and Paul reacted as all parents do in such cases. They yelled.

Surely no other child had learnt to walk as quickly or as well as their first born son! Kate beamed at her in-laws and as Paul swung his son up into the air, his dad Bernard rewound the video tape to make sure that he had captured the happy scene.

"Here, look. I just managed to get him," he said, peering into the camera monitor. Paul and Kate duly lined up. But Daniel was too pleased with his new found legs to stay still for long.

He pulled himself up again and took off in a different direction, although it was by no means certain that it was a deliberate action, more likely the pull of gravity as he tottered.

Bernard grabbed the camera again, as Kate dropped onto her knees to try to clear his path, removing the little cars, the dribble-filled teething ring, the building bricks. But she wasn't quick enough to pull the foot stool out of the way.

Daniel just caught the edge of it, and toppled over, but somehow managed to regain his balance in mid-air and, straightening up, continued on his journey of discovery.

It was not till later that afternoon that Bernard put the video into the machine and they all sat down with a cup of tea to enjoy a replay of the day's event. There Daniel was pulling himself up on the sofa, there he was taking off again. And then there he was, crashing into the foot stool..

But he didn't regain his balance on his own.

On the video, an elderly woman bent down into the picture and a protective hand was reached out to stop Daniel from falling. She pulled him straight again and with a little pat on his bottom, she sent him on his way again.

It would be hard to explain the reaction in the room. We all sit down to watch our own home videos and none of us ever expect to see anything that wasn't there when we were filming, an extra person.

At first, the four blamed it on the camera, then on the video, but there was nothing else which was out of the ordinary. The rest of the video was perfectly clear and normal. Perfectly free of surprises. The four of them eventually had to admit that this was no image from a faulty tape.

The woman on the video was perfectly clear, solid, and her movements were deliberate. There was a moment of silence as they each tried to register what it was that they had seen, then pandemonium broke out.

"Oh, my goodness, what was that?"

"Did you see that, what on earth?"

"Daniel, come here right now..."

The video was re-wound, and they watched it again. There she was. An old woman, dressed in black in the sort of clothes worn at the turn of the century. She was wearing a small, black hat with little rosebuds around its rim. There was no doubt about it. The image was crystal clear. Behind her, Kate could be seen, picking up a toy and the TV was droning away in the background.

The thing that they found hardest to cope with was the way she seemed so real, so normal. Perhaps it would have been easier to accept if she fitted in to their idea of "ghosts", perhaps if she had been see-through, or draped in chains and rags...

There was very little they could do. They watched the video literally dozens of times. They showed it to a friend of theirs who took videos professionally; they showed it to Kate's sister, Linda. But the conclusion was always the same. They had somehow managed to capture something, someone, on film, that just wasn't there.

It is hard to imagine what you would do yourself in such circumstances. Call the radio stations, TV, tabloids? Not really. This was their son, and apart from fearing ridicule and unwanted publicity, the little old lady was not something that they wanted to exploit. The image caught their imagination, but the simple gesture - saving Daniel from a fall - also tugged at their emotions.

After a few months, they met and decided to

erase the video. It was almost with a sigh of relief that they played the blank tape back to see nothing but snow and hiss.

The years passed and Paul and Kate moved house, wondering to themselves whether the "lady" would be left behind.

Daniel was eight years old by then and they had kept the story very quiet, afraid of seeing amusement in their new friends' eyes.

One night, stuck for a babysitter, a friend of theirs offered to stay with Daniel and his younger sister. Normally, Kate was reluctant to leave the kids with someone they didn't know too well but Mike was in his 30s and quite responsible.

When they came back home, the first questions were the normal ones: "How were the kids? Everything OK? Did Daniel wake up for some water? Did Holly go to the loo before she went to sleep?"

Mike mumbled some platitudes, but said very little until Kate had gone upstairs to make sure that the children were tucked in properly.

Paul poured Mike a drink and they both sank into the armchairs.

"Paul, em; this is a lovely house. Quite old, isn't it?" Mike probed. "I just thought, em, you know, whether you had ever seen anything strange?" Paul caught the strange tone of his question pretty quick considering how late it was. "What kind of strange?"

"Well," Mike continued, with a look up the stairs to make sure that Kate was out of earshot. "I was just watching television, and I saw something out of the corner of my eye. And when I turned round there was this woman. This little, old woman, dressed in black, knitting. There, in that chair in the corner. Just sitting there knitting. It was incredible. I mean, she just ignored me, as though she was the one who was meant to be here and not me. A hat? Yes, she was wearing one of those funny Mary Poppins type hats, with little flowers round the rim. But Paul, she sat there for ages..."

The little old lady has not been seen again since then. Kate's sister, Linda, has since been to see a clairvoyant, who told her that she has a guide, probably her great, great grandmother, who is taking care of her and of another family member whose name starts with a "D".

Timely Warning

Claudia wiped her hands on the tea-towel, and swept the chopped vegetables into the strainer. It was a quiet morning. Her seven-month-old daughter, Victoria, was asleep in her stroller in the middle of the hall and every now and then, she threw a glance at her through the kitchen door.

Victoria had always found it easier to fall asleep if she was being pushed up and down and she loved the stroller. She would spend hours just sitting sedately in it, watching the world go by around her.

That particular morning, she was as quiet as a mouse. Claudia finished cleaning up the vegetable peelings and then, suddenly, out of the corner of her eye, she spotted someone going up the hallway stairs.

She turned quickly in alarm in time to see a pair of men's legs disappear up the stairs. The man was wearing trousers in a dark, heavy material with turnups, and he was wearing dark, short boots. He seemed to go up the stairs slowly, measuring each step.

Claudia registered all the details in a split-second, before coming to a rapid conclusion: it was a burglar.

She was terrified. Living in a quiet village, the door was hardly ever locked but she rarely worried about the danger of anyone coming into the house, especially when she was actually there. At first, she froze, unable to think clearly, but her adrenaline was pumping up her courage. The thought of Victoria, asleep and vulnerable, in the hallway spurred her to action.

She looked at the knife she had just been using, but quickly discounted it and rummaged around in one of the drawers for something to use to protect herself and her child.

Some months before, her husband Michael had sawn the legs off a table to make it lower. One of the legs was still in the drawer. She remembered how often she had teased him about throwing it away. She sent up a mental prayer that he had taken no notice of her. It was the perfect weapon.

As she grabbed it, and edged to the doorway, she heard the telephone give a slight tinkle.

"Oh, goodness," she thought. "He's cut the phone-line."

In her panic, she had forgotten that the phone had not even been working that morning.

There was no option. She would try to grab Victoria and make a run for the back door.

She waited for a few seconds to pluck up courage, holding her breath but as soon as she got into the hallway, her panic suddenly evaporated.

Victoria was not asleep. She had somehow managed to rock the stroller up against the wall and was busy stuffing flowers and leaves from a poinsettia into her mouth.

Claudia was stunned. Her daughter's mouth was full of red petals and white sap was running down her chin. Some of the leaves had obviously started to choke her and she was trying to cough them up. There was not a moment to lose.

Even now, years later, Claudia describes the next seconds with all the intensity of the actual moment. She says that she was filled with an absolute calm. At that moment, she knew - just knew - that the man had not been any burglar. It had been her grandfather, a doctor who had died years before she herself had been born.

She could not begin to explain why she is so sure but there is no doubt in her mind. Had he not alerted her, she would have never realised that her daughter was in danger. Rather than frighten her, the ghost had saved Victoria's life.

The next few minutes were a frenzy of activity. Claudia swept the child up into her arms, terrified that she was either going to choke or get poisoned by the leaves and sap.

As she flung open the door, intending to dash down the road to a neighbour to find help, she rushed headlong into a telephone company engineer. He looked at her in bemused surprise.

"It's all right, *sinjura*. The telephone is fixed."

It was only then that she realised that the little tinkle she had heard was the telephone being reconnected.

She breathed a sigh of relief. There was no time to waste. The engineer took care of Victoria while she called emergency and waited for the ambulance. She went upstairs to get a few things that Victoria might need in the hospital: a sweater; a blanket; her changing bag. It never occurred to her to look for the mystery man. She knew that she would not find anyone.

Within an hour the drama was over. Victoria had been taken care of at the hospital and was pronounced fine although the doctors agreed that she had probably been saved in the nick of time.

Claudia did not volunteer information on how she had been alerted to the danger.

Later that evening, when she was sitting down with her husband Michael, she commented that it was a good thing that he had reported the telephone fault as it had been vital in that sort of emergency.

"But I forgot to call Telemalta, actually," he admitted sheepishly.

Claudia looked out into the hallway. It was silent and dark. Was it possible that....?

Claudia will never know for sure who she saw going up the stairs, but she is sure that her grandfather is Victoria's self-designated guardian. She sleeps easier at night, knowing that he is up there, keeping a careful eye on her.

Canine Kindness

This is not the only time that an unexplained presence turned out to be a Good Samaritan.

George was just a young toddler in the war, living in what remained of the bombed-out Three Cities. His mother was waiting anxiously for the convoy that was rumoured to be on its way.

Times had been so tough, there was no food at all to be had anywhere. She had given up walking miles just to find an egg. All they seemed to eat were carob pods. They had even had to resort to eating

9

dogs but there were none left.

The whole population seemed to be on the edge of starvation, waiting, waiting, waiting for the convoy to arrive with salvation.

But George's mother could not bear it any longer. She could not stand to look at her little son, his frame thin and scrawny in spite of the fact that she would go for days without food to give him all she could find.

She fell to her knees and prayed, her hands pressed together, her eyes shut.

When she opened her eyes, a dog appeared at the open front door. His coat seemed to glow with good health. Where had he come from?

And in his jaws the dog had a steaming loaf of freshly-baked bread. He laid it at the toddler's feet and trotted off again.

George's mother is convinced that it was a miracle. There were hardly any dogs left around and certainly even the most clever stray would not be able to scrounge enough scraps to keep itself alive and in such good shape.

And bread? What dog would find a loaf of bread and give it up?

And anyway it was ages since she had seen anything like normal flour. Where would the dog have found a whole loaf?

George's mother did not care. Wherever the gift had come from, she accepted it with the sign of the cross.

Message in the Painting

Guy always looked forward to his weekends in Berkshire. Philip was a good pal, and they always managed to fill the time. And if that included a few parties, well, they were 19-year-olds after all…

That particular weekend was just before Christmas and it had been a party to end all parties. Finally everyone had gone to bed and Guy and Philip sat down in front of the fire, finishing off the last dregs of drink. They were at that stage of inebriation when mellowness sets in, and Guy wandered unsteadily up to the fire to warm his hands. He was only half listening to Philip's musings and for some reason, the painting over the mantelpiece caught his eye. He must have looked at that painting dozens of times before, but this time, he noticed it properly.

It was a watercolour of a lovely Georgian mansion. At the bottom of the picture, there were massive gates at the end of a sweeping gravel drive, which looked about a quarter of a mile long. The name of the house was partially hidden by the trees. "…lock Hall" is all that was visible.

The house at the end of the drive nestled welcomingly among stately trees, with a more modern wing added at one end.

It was this wing which caught Guy's attention.

He interrupted Philip: " Hey, did you ever notice that the French windows are open? Here in the picture?"

Philip looked at him blankly.

"Funny, I never noticed before."

Philip ignored his friend and Guy went back to sprawl on the sofa. Soon later, they went to bed.

The next morning, Guy remembered the picture and when they went down to breakfast, he wandered over to the painting again. He peered closely, not quite believing his eyes.

The French windows were closed.

Philip laughed off the whole thing.

"Come on, Guy. We had quite a skinful last night. You probably imagined the whole thing."

Even though Guy was convinced about what he had seen, he admitted that his argument was not exactly on firm ground, and he sat down to pore over the newspaper.

He read a small item about the death of the eldest son of an influential family. The paper said that the mysterious death was the last in a long series of tragedies which had befallen the family, whose sons died before they reached puberty.

Guy turned over to the sports section. At 19, a hangover takes precedence over mystery.

Guy went down to stay with his friend regularly over the next few years. But it was only four years later that the picture caught his attention again.

It was the week before Christmas and once again he and Philip were sitting in front of the fire at around two in the morning. Guy stared at the picture and suddenly leapt to his feet and ran over to scrutinise it.

"Philip! Look at this!" he almost yelled. "There is a spot on the picture!"

Philip laughed.

"You and that blessed picture! What do you mean there is a spot?" he asked. He ambled over to the picture and peered at it. And then, spitting on his finger, rubbed over the glass, convinced that it was just some dirt. The spot was still there.

Perhaps it was just too late at night. But Philip was in no mood for another discussion about the picture.

"It is probably the picture itself, some damp or something."

Once again, the picture was forgotten...

...until the next morning, when Guy went down to breakfast and picked up the paper. He read about the eldest son of an established family who was seriously ill. The family, he read, had lost several eldest sons to the mysterious illness.

Guy suddenly shuddered. He had just remembered the snippet he had read in the paper four years before. Even though he had barely paid any attention to it at the time, he could now see it clearly again in his mind.

The same family - another sick child.

Even now, recounting the story after 30 years, Guy shook with the vivid recollection of that dreadful night. Telling the story, he paced restlessly up and down, hands waving in the air to show the urgency, the obsessive feeling which had swept over him.

Because he suddenly knew, he just knew that the picture was somehow related to that family's curse.

Philip was watching him with some surprise as he threw down the paper and ran to the fireplace.

But even Philip had to admit that the spot was still there.

And it had moved.

The spot was now on the inside of the gates.

Guy could not explain the shiver of terror which ran down his spine, yet he knew he had to do something about the picture. They phoned the newspaper offices where someone promised to try to find out more about the family. The rest of the day passed by in a daze. And when the phone finally rang in the evening, Guy could hardly control himself. Philip put the phone back in its cradle and looked at Guy in amazement.

"The family lives in Exmoor," he said, "and the

name of the house is Porlock Hall."

If there had been any doubt in their minds, the name of the house dispelled it. But what could they do? It was at least four hours' drive to Exmoor. The fact that the two got into Philip's car and drove off, the picture laid carefully on the back seat, was the best proof of how strongly they were possessed by the feeling of impending doom.

It was six in the evening and already dark, a light rain was falling as they set off, which rapidly grew heavier and heavier.

It was no night to be out and certainly not on a wild goose chase. And yet...whenever they asked themselves whether they were mad or not, they looked at the picture again.

The spot was still moving inexorably down the drive in the picture.

The rain turned to sleet and then a blinding snowstorm. The trees were being whipped by gale force winds as the two men peered anxiously through the windscreen, each sweep of the wipers barely clearing the screen long enough for them to see where they were going.

The car sped and skidded its way to Exmoor, stopping only long enough for them to ask directions.

The minutes seemed interminable and each time they looked at the picture the spot had moved.

By the time they got to Porlock Hill, the spot was just outside the French windows.

The hill was steep, one in four, and the car's tires could hardly get a grip on the icy roads. But Guy and Philip did not get the chance to notice where they were. Ahead of them, looming through the blinding storm, they finally saw Porlock Hall. It had never even occurred to them that it might not be the house in the picture. So they did not even stop to wonder at the by now familiar gates but sped down the drive in a crunch of gravel.

As they skidded to a halt, the beam of the headlights reflected brightly off the glass in the window-panes ahead of them, breaking into hundreds of pin-points on each snowflake.

The spot on the picture had reached the French windows and as they drove, they heard a little crack. The windows burst open, both in the picture and before their very eyes. The spot was disappearing inside.

They leapt out of the car, and ran through the windows, not even stopping to think what they must have looked like, two dishevelled lads, total strangers, bursting into an ancestral home in the middle of a stormy night.

They made their way upstairs, vaguely aware that someone in one of the rooms called out to them: "They're upstairs!"

They burst into a bedroom, to find a family clustered around the bed of a seriously ill eight-year-old boy, who was clearly on his deathbed.

As they watched in stunned silence the boy's fever broke and, under the eyes of all those present, ebbed away. His colour returned.

The end of the story is almost an anti-climax. Guy and Philip explained to the family what they had seen on the picture. They accepted the explanation, unable to deny the inexplicable tragedies of the past or the sudden recovery of their son.

For several years, they kept in touch with the grateful family. The picture was put up again over Philip's mantelpiece where it still is today. The spot had disappeared, never to reappear again.

And the French windows have remained tightly closed.

Guy never found an explanation for the picture nor any link to the cursed household. Perhaps, he felt, it would be better not to ask too much.

Relative Values

Nadia was a fairly down to earth child. For a 12-year-old, she was quite sensible in most normal situations, but this was hardly a normal situation.

She had been fast asleep but something disturbed her. She was a very light sleeper, but when she woke up, the only noise she sensed was the sound of light footsteps on the wooden floor-tiles leading to their room.

Nadia sat up and looked at her sister's bed next to hers, thinking perhaps that she had gone to the bathroom, but Daniella was still there fast asleep.

Nadia could feel the hairs on the back of her neck rise. It was a spooky house at the best of times, with high ceilings striped with shadows, and the sort of creaks and cracks that old houses use to keep you on edge.

So Nadia was already feeling quite frightened when the woman walked into her bedroom. At first, she thought - hoped - that it was her mother, but the woman was much slimmer than her mother. She was wearing a long, white dress, a bit like a nightie, and she was wearing glasses. She did not seem old, perhaps in her 30s, and she certainly did not look frightening. But that did not stop Nadia from screaming as loud as she could. The woman ignored the screaming and continued walking into the room. As soon as she reached Daniella's bed, which was the closest to the door, she vanished.

By now, the whole household was awake, and it took some time for them to calm Nadia down. Daniella seemed unperturbed by the thought of a ghost walking straight through her, but Nadia was really shaken up.

Still, what could the family do? They were hardly going to move out of the house on the basis of a 10-second vision.

Time passed and the fear subsided, somewhat at any rate. A year later, a Maltese friend who lived in the UK decided to visit. She spent seven days in the house, sharing Nadia's room with her, instead of Daniella. But from the moment she walked through the door, she shivered.

"There is something in this house," she announced.

The family paid no attention. She was what you would describe as "sensitive" if you were kind, but "eccentric" if you were not.

For the whole of her stay, she would report every morning that she had heard footsteps outside the room. There was a very old leather bench in the corridor outside the room. And she would hear, very, very clearly, the creak and crack of the leather and wood as the ghost sat down. It would sit quietly for a short time and then, just as clearly, she would hear the creaking noises as the ghost got up and walked away.

And the family were still sceptical. Until Nadia's other sister Christine also saw something, this time a woman wearing a raincoat.

Today, the vivid terror of that moment still haunts her. Now 27, just the mention of the ghost transports Christine back through time to the 10-year-old child she once was.

"It was years ago," she said, her voice lowering involuntarily to a whisper. "But I will never forget."

The young girl had also been in bed when she heard a creaking in the old house, provoking unnerving echoes of her sister's experience.

"I thought it was my mother... She would often come in to check on us. I knew the sounds of the house and it just seemed like mother walking around."

Wide awake with expectation, Christine leaned up on her pillow.

"Then I saw her, not my mother, but a sort of ageless woman wearing a white coat. Her hair was bobbed and she was wearing a blue polo neck. The whole apparition was so vivid," she recalled.

What happened next, Christine does not know The poor girl gripped her head in her hands, closed her eyes tightly and waited for the woman to go away. Shocked by the experience, she was unable to sleep that night.

"I have never seen anything like it since. You ask do I believe in ghosts? Of course I do."

The haunting sent shivers through the household and every noise, no matter how slight, was interpreted as the restless movements of the wandering spirit.

One evening, the ghost seemed more restless than usual. Nadia's parents had gone out and left the children with a friend. The children had gone to bed some time before and the babysitter was relaxing, sitting in bed, reading. She then heard someone playing the piano.

She thought that one of the girls had woken up

and gone downstairs, but when she checked she found they were all in their beds. When she peered over the banister, the rooms downstairs were all dark.

Summoning up her courage, she started to venture down the stairs, one wary footstep at a time.

The sounds from the old instrument continued to sweep through the house. Suddenly, without explanation, the music stopped. The house returned to the normal sleepy sounds of the night; but the babysitter's pulse continued to race.

And so time passed and the family were no closer to finding out the truth about the strange woman who seemed so attached to them. None of their neighbours had ever heard about the house being haunted and there were no traumas or tragedies attached to the house.

The whole chilling chapter appeared to be closed. Then one day, Nadia was sifting through a box of old photographs with her mother when she came across a picture of a woman. Nadia's face froze.

Not noticing the change in her daughter's expression, her mother said:
"That's your father's mother, the Scottish one."

She gently took the photo from Nadia's hands and murmured: "Unfortunately she died in Scotland and never got the chance to meet you."

She then realised that Nadia was staring at the photo, her mouth open, her eyes full of tears.

"That's her. That's the ghost I saw," she said. "She was even wearing the same glasses."

It seemed the grandmother did get the chance to be with her grandchildren after all.

Sibling Ties

Paula was only one and a half years old when her teenage brother, Michael, was killed in a traffic accident, so she didn't remember him at all. Her grieving parents, Josephine and Alex, found any reference to him terribly painful and soon after the accident, all the photos of him were silently removed, one by one. His room was cleared out, and the door of his room was pulled quietly shut as his parents tried to get on with their lives.

Paula was a happy, contented child, growing up unaware of the void left in the family. Bouncy with long dark hair, she was as pretty and uncaring a child as one could imagine.

But somehow, she seemed to sense that there was someone missing.

Once when she was walking down Republic Street, in Valletta on a shopping trip with her mum, she slipped her hand in her mother's in the natural spontaneous way that children have. Then she reached out her hand as if to take someone else's. Her mother was surprised.

"Whose hand are you holding?" she asked, thinking that Paula would say an imaginary friend. But she was not prepared for the innocent reply.

"It's my brother."

Her words stopped Josephine dead in her tracks.

Two years had passed by then, but the wound had hardly even started to heal. Perhaps this was why she did not pursue the matter. She just turned quietly away to regain her composure and carried on walking.

But Paula carried on slipping her hand into that

of an imaginary person whenever they went out.

Time ticked by and Paula grew older, going to playgroup and behaving just like any pre-schooler, but something happened which was to change her life.

The family was going through a tough time after the bereavement. There were constant fights and Paula listened to them from her bedroom, terrified that her world was to be torn apart. She started having nightmares.

She would wake up screaming and scared and her parents could do little to calm her down.

Then one night, when Josephine went into the child's bedroom after a nightmare, she found her already calm. She was sitting up on her bed whispering to someone. Josephine did not ask her who it was. Somehow, she wasn't sure that she wanted to know.

Still, the nightmares gradually petered out, whether because of her 'friend' or not, Josephine did not dare find out.

But it was no longer just at night that Paula started to have her whispered conversations. One day, Josephine went to tuck her in for an afternoon nap and sat on the edge of the bed. And Paula pushed her away.

"You can't sit there, ma. That's where Michael sits."

It had been almost four years since he had been killed, but no parent ever gets over the loss of a child. Josephine was torn. She was sceptical about the inexplicable. But at the same time, someone inside her wanted to believe that it was really him, that some part of him was still there.

At the same time, she was not sure whether this

21

was a good or bad thing for Paula. And Josephine didn't dare mention it to Alex. Although he rarely showed his feelings, the loss of his beloved son had changed him forever.

Whatever Paula could see, it became more often.

She was once sitting at the kitchen table, poring over her homework. Her tongue was sticking out of the side of her mouth as she concentrated on her sums. She got stuck on one, rubbing out the answer, then trying again. With a little sigh of exasperation, she rubbed it out again. Then she turned to her side, had a little whispered conversation, and wrote down the answer. Obviously this time, she was content with the answer. She shut her book with a flourish, put everything back into her school backpack and went off to play. Josephine was left in the kitchen, her fingers running over the back of the chair, alone, confused by her strong emotions, feeling terribly left out.

She had no doubt that Paula really was seeing someone. But was it…?

The matter had become an obsession. Josephine thought about it all the time, and finally had to give in to her tortured curiosity. She realised that she had to know, one way or the other, no matter how painful it would be.

One day, as Paula was lying down on the ground, colouring pens spread all around her, Josephine went to sit down next to her and carefully started to prise information from her.

Paula was barely six - she didn't pick up the note of emotion in her mother's voice and quite happily described what Michael was wearing. The sneakers, the T-shirt, the shorts…. She had some trouble explaining the colour of his shorts though, looking round the room to find something the same shade. None of her colouring pens would do, then she ran triumphantly over to the curtains and pointed to a particular shade of blue.

It was proof - if Josephine needed it. They were the exact same clothes he had been wearing on that fateful day. And she knew that Paula could have had no way of knowing.

There is no ending to this story. Paula still sees her brother and he helps her get through all sorts of situations.

Josephine bears the burden of her knowledge on her own.

Who would believe her? But she knows that, for what it is worth, Michael is not completely gone.

Good Samaritan

Andrew was not used to the weather in Canada. Brought up in Malta, he had never experienced a really harsh winter, and the first snowstorm took him by surprise. Had it been a few years later, he would never have attempted the drive home from work through a snow-storm.

But he wanted to get home and took off early, hoping to get there before the worst of it struck.

The snow was a fine frosting while he was on the urban roads, but once he got out into the countryside, the full fury of the snowstorm hit him with its force.

His windscreen wipers could hardly keep up with the falling snow and he struggled to peer through it to the narrow stretch of road lit by his headlights. The street lights had long since ended, and he could not see a single light anywhere across the flat fields. He felt as if he were the last human being in the world. He could feel himself getting tense and when the car skidded off the road, he almost screamed out loud. The car skated almost gracefully sideways, ending up with a dull thud in the bank of snow along the roadside.

The engine sputtered and died. The falling snow seemed to suck all the sound out of the air, creating a thick blanket of silence. Andrew sat there in the dark for a moment. With the engine off, the car grew cold very quickly. Would the car start again? With a big sigh, he turned the key, not daring to hope. The car whined a little but did not start. He tried again. Again, just a whine. He started to panic. No-one knew where he was and his wife would not miss him for a while, until the time he would normally have arrived home. Long enough for him to die of cold.

And then he heard a tap. He stayed as still as possible to listen. Yes, there it was again. This time the tap became quite insistent. He could not see anything through the steamed up window. He pulled down his sleeve and used it to rub a circle on the inside of his window.

He could hardly believe his eyes. In the dim light of the headlights, he could see a man standing there. He could not make out his face, as he had his collar pulled up the side of his face, and a hat pulled low over his ears.

The man was pointing at the bonnet. Flustered by the accident, he did not stop to think but pulled the lever to open the bonnet. The man disappeared behind it and a few seconds later, peered back around it to give Andrew the thumbs-up sign.

Andrew rubbed his hands together to try to get some feeling back into them, and tried the ignition again. It purred to life. He sent up a quiet prayer of thanks. The bonnet shut with a muffled clunk and Andrew wound down his window again to thank the stranger.

He got out of the car, pulling his jacket up around his neck. But there was no-one, and there were no footsteps in the virgin snow.

Andrew stood there silently for a moment, but he was terrified that the engine might stop again. He got back into his car and drove away, thinking that he would soon spot a village or at least a house close by, but it was miles before he saw any lights.

Who was the stranger who had probably saved his life?

Could it have been...?

Message From Beyond The Grave

When Charles first set eyes on Grace one evening in Birkirkara, he was smitten. She looked so frail, still dressed in mourning after the untimely death of her mother just a few months before. He managed to get introduced to her through mutual friends and, before long, they were courting.

It was the start of winter, 1962. The two of them gradually built up a regular routine for their dates. After he picked her up from home, they would go off for their promenade, the Maltese traditional stroll known as a *passigjata*. They would start at the San Girgor church in Zejtun, where they would have their confessions heard by the parish priest, and would then wander onto the church parvis.

Along the side of the church is a square with trees and benches surrounding a statue of St Gregory. In front of the church are the forbidding railing of the cemetery, broken only by an iron gate.

Charles and Grace sat on their favourite bench, facing the impressive church. Their friends knew better than to disturb them as they sat there, forging the first bonds of new love. The sun was just about gone and the light was fading fast, as it does at that time of year. It would soon be time to take her home.

They were oblivious to the rest of the world going by, savouring the time together.

They were so wrapped up in each other that they hardly took any notice of the woman who came out of the cemetery.

She was dressed in black, with a veil hiding her hair, and she walked slowly, measuring each step. She had probably just visited a relative's grave, they idly thought, if you could describe the fact that they had registered her presence at all as a thought.

She walked to the far side of the square, but the couple still paid little attention to her.

At least, until she walked all the way up around the statue and came face to face with them.

Grace's face stiffened. Her voice trailed off and her fingers dug into Charles' arm. She drew her breath in sharply. Charles looked at the woman to see what had prompted his girlfriend's reaction. But all he saw was an elderly woman in her 50s, with a friendly, calm face. He did not recognise her, but he too instinctively fell silent, aware of a strange atmosphere surrounding this woman that would have made their previous chatter seem frivolous and disrespectful.

She walked closer to the couple and still Grace clung to Charles, unable to say a word. Charles could feel her tremble and he looked at the woman again, startled to realise that there was something vaguely familiar about her, perhaps her eyes.

This time, the woman looked straight at Grace, and very, very slowly, nodded her head two or three times, not smiling or frowning, but very intense, as if reassuring her that everything was all right.

She then turned to face the gate from where she had just come and started to walk away.

It was only then that Grace spoke, in a small voice, thick with emotion.

"That's my mother."

Now Charles could understand his girlfriend's sharp reaction. He had never met her mother but had seen photographs of her, when she had been younger and before her illness.

He looked again at the woman who had by then passed in front of them and was slowly making her way back to the cemetery door. They sat there on the bench, still unable to move, still unable to utter a word. After what seemed an eternity, the woman reached the gate and just disappeared through it.

Grace was by now sobbing silently at his side, thoroughly shaken by the experience. Charles squeezed her arm and ran to the cemetery gate to see where the woman had gone.

The gate was bolted and there was no one inside. Only the votive candles glowed with their flickering red lights throwing shadows onto the wilted bunches of flowers on the graves, including the one belonging to his girlfriend's mother.

He looked behind him but there was no one around, no one by the church or on the square. The woman had simply disappeared.

He ran back to Grace, who was still sitting on the bench, trying to comprehend what had happened. But her tears had by then changed into a more peaceful thoughtfulness.

"Why do you think she came?" she wondered. "Do you think she was trying to ask us to pray for her?"

"Perhaps she was trying to tell you that she is out of pain and peaceful now," suggested Charles.

The two looked at each other. Both were thinking the same thing. That they would probably have doubted their own senses had they been alone when they saw the woman.

After a brief discussion, they walked thoughtfully home and summoned the rest of her family. The deeply religious family were at first incredulous about Grace's story, but they soon accepted that it had in fact been her mother.

They all agreed to pray together, a family still in mourning, still deeply grieving their tragic loss, but reassured that she was now in good hands.

The woman was never seen again, although they went to the same bench regularly. But many times, they looked at the iron gate of the cemetery and wondered whether she was now lying peacefully.

Charles and Grace are now married. He still carries the memory of the woman who would have been his mother-in-law had she been alive. He never knew her then, but he feels that he did meet her, once, and that she had approved of him...

Lady Of The Castle

Fort St Angelo has a vast and chequered history. It was originally a castle known as Castrum Maris and its history has been charted as far back as 1241. At that time, the castle belonged to the di Nava family and was virtually the only major construction on the peninsula.

In 1530, the Knights of the Order of St John came to Malta and Grandmaster L'Isle Adam had his first residence built within the castle. It was subsequently embellished through the reign of the next two grandmasters. It was a bustling hive of activity at the time of the British, with the victualling yard and Naval Bakery based nearby. But the war changed all that, reducing much of its majesty into ruins.

The fort received 69 direct bomb hits during World War II.

The officers billeted there had been moved to new premises, as the ones they had were too far from the air-raid shelters, and a series of tunnels was set up to hold all the personnel.

By the end of 1942, the vacated dormitories were being used as a wardroom and dining room.

On this particular day, the ward was full of sick personnel. It may have been the war, but even so, ill health still struck.

The ward was allocated to those recovering from relatively prosaic problems like gastric flu, pneumonia, appendicitis. Some of the men were propped up in their beds, reading, chatting, playing cards. A few of them wandered around in their tartan dressing-gowns and slippers. All of a sudden the room went cold and still. The men looked up in surprise. The figure of a woman appeared out of nowhere at the end of the room. She floated across the air, looking at the men with a worried expression on her face, her white, flowing dress drifting behind her as light as a feather. She swept her arm anxiously in the air, as if calling the men to her.

They looked at her in stunned amazement. Was

this the famous ghost of the Grey Lady?

But the men did not have time to worry about the manifestation. The woman's gestures were becoming more and more frantic and she floated towards the doorway.

One man spoke up.

"I think she's trying to tell us something," he said. "She seems to be trying to tell us to follow her."

"Do you think we should?" asked another.

And then the woman disappeared. The men thought about it for a few seconds and then decided to follow. One by one they got out of their beds and staggered and limped their way outside.

No sooner had they walked out past the amazed nurses than a bomb fell on the ward.

A lone plane had managed to evade the anti-aircraft fire long enough to get over the Grand Harbour and drop its lethal cargo. Had the men not walked out of the ward the moment they did , they would all have been wiped out.

In his book "The Ghost of Malta", Joseph Attard traces the legend of the Grey Lady of Fort St Angelo.

He identifies the Grey Lady as one of the two women in the life of Captain di Nava. At one point, it seems that her attention became unwelcome and he ordered two of his guards to get rid of her. She was killed and her body thrown into a dungeon.

For the past 450 years, her ghost has apparently haunted the fort, seen in various places. There would be tell-tale signs: a cold blast of air, the slowly opening doors, and the rustle of skirts. Many people have reportedly seen her, including young children who describe her as beautiful but sad.

Restorations a few years ago uncovered the entrance to the dungeons, and the story goes that three skeletons were found there, two male and one female. Was it the Grey Lady's?

The Volunteer

There was very little to do to the building, Joanna thought, as she walked around the house. It would be ideal as her new school. It was 1980, and like many other houses in the area, it was about 70-years-old. With a bit of redecorating it would do just fine.

There was an elderly couple who lived upstairs, and they tended most of the garden, leaving her just a small yard and access to a small cellar. But after all, that was all she needed. She certainly didn't want the trouble of looking after the garden, and the elderly couple had perfectly adequate green fingers.

She hired a painter to do most of the decorating and work was progressing quite smoothly. One evening, though, she was rather surprised to find him waiting outside on the pavement for her when she arrived. He was covered in plaster and splashes of whitewash. His bags of tools were packed, lying on the ground by his feet, and he was obviously quite upset.

"Gianni, what has happened? Don't tell me you already have to leave today?" Joanna wailed, knowing from experience that workmen have their own inexplicable timetable when it comes to starting and finishing jobs.

"No, sinjura. No. I can't work here any more. I'm sorry, sinjura, but I can't. You have ghosts here. I had better not tell you what I saw, but I tell you, there is no way you will get me back in there," he sobbed. He said he had run out of the house so fast that he had knocked over a woman and her pushchair on the pavement.

Joanna sighed. This was one problem she could do without. She had dozens of other things to do, but she managed to persuade Gianni to go back and continue working by promising to stay with him all the time he was there.

She spent several days sitting in the rooms with him while he worked, at his insistence. She knitted to pass the time, feeling quite comfortable in the house. She was completely unconvinced by his story, and when he finished the job, she was irritated that she had had to waste so much time because of what was obviously a fervent imagination.

He refused to tell her what it was that he had seen though. She concluded that he had probably heard noises coming from the cellar. The thought crossed her mind that it was a closed room and that no voices from outside the building could have filtered through.

But she soon dismissed her doubts and didn't give the matter another thought, anxious to get on with all the other work she needed to get through before the school opened.

Years went by without incident. The school prospered and students soon filled all the rooms. They started to run out of space, especially for storage.

The cellar could only be reached from the yard, down four or five steps, so it was not really very convenient, but eventually they were forced to start using it as a storeroom. A louvred door allowed air to circulate and there wasn't much damp.

Then the couple upstairs started to complain that there were rats in the cellar. Joanna was very sceptical; after all, she had never found any droppings and none of the paper and books stored there showed any signs of vermin. But to humour them, she put some rat poison down and pulled the louvred doors shut, pulling an old stone bench across the door. She hated rat poison and was terrified that some student might go into the cellar and find it.

But one of her teachers was quite surprised when she saw her dragging the heavy bench.

"But if you put that there, what is going to happen to the man who lives down there?" she asked.

Joanna looked at her blankly.

"Lives where?"

"The old man, you know, the one who wears a checked shirt... Well, I say he lives there, he is always working down there, pottering around," she explained.

Joanna was stunned. Her teacher explained that she saw the man regularly. She just assumed that he worked for the people upstairs. There was obviously nothing menacing about him - the teacher seemed to regard him as quite a benevolent character.

Who could the man be? Joanna knew that the couple upstairs did their own gardening, and after all the cellar was full of the school stores, so whoever it was could not be using the cellar. But she checked with the people upstairs anyway. No, they didn't have any handyman or gardener. "And anyway, even if we did, why should he use *your* cellar?" they asked.

Her first thought was to keep the story quiet. The last thing she wanted was to alarm the students. She persuaded the teacher that the man had only been there temporarily, and tried to forget about it. She herself was often alone in the house in the evenings, and it had such a happy, sunny feel. She couldn't afford to let her imagination get the better of her.

Months went by. A student was sitting down with her in her office late one afternoon, waiting to be picked up after a lesson, and they ran out of small chat. The girl tried to find something to talk about to fill the silence before it became awkward.

"I haven't seen the gardener for a while," she said.

Joanna did not look up from her paperwork and merely mumbled acknowledgement. But as she realised what the girl had said, her heart sank.

"Gardener? Who do you mean?"

"The one that used to come to water the garden. You know. The one who always wore a checked shirt. Such a nice man. He always used to smile when he saw me. Did he retire? He wasn't that old, though. Perhaps he's sick or something," she twittered on.

Joanna almost sighed out aloud in relief when she heard the girl's mother hoot her horn outside. She sat there in the quiet building for a while, musing over the man who had been seen by so many people. A man she knew did not exist, not in flesh and blood anyway.

She never did find out any more about him. The school is still in use and she has never heard of any more encounters with the strange man in the checked shirt.

Tenacious Tenant

Jennifer was not ready to sleep alone. She was only five-years-old and her older sister's rhythmic breathing was a great comforter. And through the open door of her bedroom, she could see her parents' room across the corridor.

But one night, something happened which was to terrify her, something which caused her to fear dark nights for years to come.

She was woken up by something – she does not remember it as noise, rather as a presence. When she opened her eyes, she felt something behind her and leapt down to the bottom of her bed. When she turned around, she saw an elderly woman hunched over her shoulders. The woman seemed to be hovering in the air, with both her arms outstretched, fingers clawed towards her. She was old and gaunt, although not ugly. She did what any five-year-old would do. She screamed.

Jennifer clambered off the end of her bed and ran across the corridor. Her sister woke up, startled, and also leapt out of bed and towards her parents' room. Because it was dark, her eyes had not yet focused and Jennifer saw her pass straight through the ghostly image. Her sister felt the icy coldness as she passed and it was only then that she turned around, by then fully awake, and saw the woman.

Jennifer's mother jumped out of her bed as soon as she heard the screaming, and met Jennifer in the corridor. Her hand instinctively went for the light switch and she suddenly found herself with one screaming child under each arm.

"It's all right," she muttered. "You've just had a nightmare." But the girls could not be soothed. Both swore that they had seen the woman and that her image had been sucked under a chair and faded into nothingness as soon as the light had gone on.

The mother did her best to calm them down, but both the girls were haunted by the image they knew they had seen. For years, Jennifer was unable to sleep properly.

The ghost was never seen again. And yet her sister says that their cats would often get wild when she was preparing their food. All their fur would rise and they would start dashing this way and that, trying to get out of the house whichever way they could. Various other odd things happened, but nothing that could not be explained away.

When she was about 12, the family moved. It was then, and only then, that her mother admitted that she too had seen the ghost that night. She had never said anything about it because the girls had obviously been upset enough. But she too had been upset. After all, she knew who the woman was.

Years before, she and her husband had been looking for a house to buy and had gone to see a house in Sliema. The couple who lived there had decided to emigrate to Canada and had made all their plans and arrangements. But her mother still lived in the house, old and frail and in need of constant attention. They could not bear to put her into a home and so had decided to wait until she died.

But she lingered and lingered, wavering on the edge of death, and they were beginning to worry about whether the opportunities in Canada would soon slip away. The love that kept them from putting her into a home was turning into ill-concealed impatience.

But eventually, the old lady died and they left, passing the house over to Jennifer's parents. But the old lady's spirit must have lingered just a while longer, for it was her image that Jennifer's mother had recognised.

Jennifer's mother had another experience with the

'other world'. When she was young, a few years before the war, she used to go to her favourite godmother's for tea. At that time, a ouija board was all the rage, and they would often tinker with it, perhaps not fully aware of what they were doing. They were probably totally surprised and terrified when the board started 'responding'. The spirit warned, letter by letter, that her godmother should have the ceiling checked.

They were totally bewildered. Why would a spirit contact them with such a prosaic request? But her god-mother felt that it must be important and had an architect brought in. He carefully surveyed the ceiling and said that it was not in need of any major restoration, but the godmother insisted and various works were carried out.

Both Jennifer's mother and her godmother were in the house during a series of air-raids once the war started. The endless bombardment sent shock-waves through the row of houses. The tremors finally proved too much for the old buildings and they collapsed, all except for the godmoth-er's. Thanks to the re-enforced ceiling, it withstood the shocks.

The Call

When her newborn daughter was put into her arms, Jackie's eyes filled with tears. Such tiny fin-gers, such peaceful innocence...

It took a long time for her to accept that the child had a congenital heart defect. Paula lived for six years, during which time she underwent surgery and treatment, but eventually she succumbed to complications and left Jackie and her family grieving over their tragic loss.

Life goes on, no matter how empty it may seem, and Jackie had another daughter, two years younger, who also needed her. They gradually put back together the pieces of their life and a few years later, in the early 1980s, they moved to Holland.

It was tough settling in to a new country at first, and the family concentrated on moving their possessions into the house to make it a home. They always seemed to be busy, but there was one afternoon when Jackie realised that the house was silent.

It was a rare treat. Her toddler son was asleep, her husband was dozing on the sofa and her daughter, Caroline, was reading. She pottered around the kitchen, relishing the peace.

And then the phone rang.

It seemed louder than normal that afternoon, jangling in the uncanny quiet.

Caroline looked at her dad, and realising that he was asleep, picked the phone up herself.

From the kitchen, Jackie could hear her say 'hello' a few times, and wondered idly whether it was an overseas call from home, still put through by the operator in those days. After all, they really didn't know anyone in Holland yet.

Caroline's voice faltered. "Sophie, is that you?" she asked, thinking that it was her cousin.

And then she went quiet.

"Mum, can you come here, quickly..." she said in an unnaturally tense voice.

Jackie walked over to the phone, and looked questioningly at her daughter, but Caroline refused to look her in the eye. She took the receiver and put it to her ear, not sure what to expect.

The static on the line hissed, and she could vaguely make out the sound of children's voices in the background. She assumed that it was an overseas connection, until the line suddenly cleared and a voice came clearly, if somewhat distantly, across the line.

"Hello."

"Is that you, Sophie?" she asked. But she could feel a tingle work its way up her spine.

"No, mummy. It's me," the voice said, a voice which sounded just like Paula's.

And then the child on the other end of the line giggled, and Jackie could feel her legs weaken under her. There was no mistaking that familiar sound, etched into her memory.

"Mummy," the voice insisted. "It's me, Paula..."

And then the line cut dead.

Jackie stood there for an eternity, unable to move. The sudden turmoil of emotions made her incapable of even putting down the receiver.

She looked at Caroline, who was also rooted to the spot.

"Who was that?"

She still couldn't look her mother in the eye. "I don't know."

Jackie could not quite come to terms with it. For three weeks, she could not bring herself to answer the phone, torn between fear and hope that it might be her dead daughter again. She tried to find a logical explanation but who else could it have been? She didn't know anyone in Holland, certainly no-one who would have known about Paula. And a prank? Who would have done such a thing?

And then there was the giggle, that beloved, unmistakable giggle. The only thing that kept her from believing that she had somehow imagined the whole thing, perhaps through delayed grief, was that she knew that Caroline had also recognised the voice, even though she refused flatly to discuss it

Jackie has spent years trying to get in touch with other people who have received phone-calls from beyond the grave. Most of the people she traced had received phone-calls from a close relative, just a seemingly normal chat, only to find out that the person had died a few hours before. She has never heard of anyone else receiving a call four years later. It was not even a significant date, birthday or anniversary. Was Paula just calling to let her mother know that she was OK?

That was the conclusion that Jackie came to, after many years of soul-searching, a conclusion that finally let her put the episode behind her.

Until last year, when Caroline finally admitted that she too had recognised her sister.

The Hotel Guest

The former general manager of one of Malta's leading hotels used to work in a hotel in London. In 1991, a guest came to him with an unusual request. This is the story he told me.

It was not an unusual afternoon for a busy London hotel. I was in the lobby watching the comings and goings in the busy bar. Middle eastern and western businessmen, weary travellers, checking in after everlasting long-haul flights... there seemed to be so much going on.

I was with our chief of security, a burly 6ft tall former police inspector called Burrows.

A lady who was obviously one of the guests came over to us: "You're Mr Burrows, aren't you?" He looked at her, not recognising her, but his polite look of interest soon turned to amazement. The lady was none other than Betty Shine, a well known healer and psychic.

She and her husband Alan had gone to sleep in their room the previous night, but at around 3am, she had been woken up by the sound of rattling ice-cubes.

Next to the ice-bucket in the corner, she made out the shape of a spirit, holding the bucket and shaking it for all its worth. She shook her husband awake, but he wearily assured her that there was nobody there.

He was used to Betty: she had already written several books about her experiences with healing and psychic phenomena.

Betty waited and, sure enough, the spirit started to communicate with her. He explained that he had died of a heart attack in that very hotel. She described him as being in great distress. She approached Burrows to find out whether he remembered the case.

Burrows did not believe in the paranormal, dismissing these things as 'absolute rubbish'. But this story really disturbed him – he realised that the story must be true as he had been the one to get the dead man out of the room, just down the very same corridor in which Betty Shine was staying.

The man had died three years before to the very month. In spite of his tough exterior, the incident had really shaken Burrows – and he had done his best to forget all about it.

The story spread through the hotel like wildfire, and the staff were all curious to find out more. Wherever Betty went the next morning, curious eyes followed her, whether at breakfast or in the foyer. But till then, there was little more to tell.

The next night however, she was again woken

up by the man's ghost rattling the ice-bucket. This time she described him as being in his late 40s, with dark hair and quite good looking.

He explained the cause of his distress: he had not said goodbye to his daughters and he wanted to speak to them. He gave Betty part of an address and disappeared. His request was simple: to tell his daughters that he was all right, that they should get on with their lives.

The next morning, she duly passed the address on to Burrows, and even though incomplete, he knew it to be correct as he had had to contact the aunt who had lived there after the man's death.

Burrows admitted that his scepticism was being sorely tested – the details that she had recounted were all exact. Could she have found them out from anywhere else? Burrows certainly did not think so. The files on the case were – as are all guests' – confidential, and the death had not attracted undue publicity at the time.

It emerged that the man had only been in England on a visit, and his two daughters had actually been waiting downstairs in the hotel lobby for him. The reunion never took place.

When he failed to show up after an hour, the security guard had gone up to the man's room with the two daughters, and he had been found dead in the bath.

I spoke to Betty Shine myself at length not just about this incident, but also about various places she had visited. She did explain that only 'sensitive' people would be able to make contact with spirits, but I did ask her to play down the incident. Both staff and guests were quite concerned.

Betty and Burrows talked about the incident and

decided that the spirit wanted to pass on his message to the daughters, but to this day, he never had the heart to do it.

Is the man's spirit still in distress? Perhaps not.

Or perhaps he has still not been able to find anyone to pass on his message...

The incident was subsequently mentioned, with some changes, in Ms. Shine's next book.

CHAPTER TWO

One of the many theories about ghosts is that they are vestiges of energy, echoes of the person that once lived. A Scottish friend lived in a house on the edge of an old castle, and she said that with amazing regularity, a sentry, complete with sentry box, would appear in the garden outside their kitchen window. The whole neighbourhood, vicar and all, knew about the sentry and had often seen him there, shuffling his feet to keep warm. My friend would look out of the window and see her mother bending down doing some weeding, right in the centre of the apparition, but totally unaware of him. He never did anything different, just the same sequence of events played over and over again. My friend said that he appeared whenever there was a particular combination of cold and damp. Is that all that ghosts are? An echo?

In these stories, the apparition seems to have become attached to a building, repeating some habitual action over and over again, oblivious to the fact that there are witnesses to the ritual…

Reaching Out

The town of Datchet in Berkshire is perhaps not too well known, although its proximity to Windsor makes it a convenient watering-hole for the thirsty.

It has been that way for years, hundreds of years. Lying along the side of the Thames, it has always been a stopping point for travellers and a tavern stood on the site at the time of the Domesday Book.

In a country famous for its historic pubs, inns and taverns, the tavern at Datchet does not offer anything special in the way of architecture. Its bay windows, with their small wooden panels, are pretty enough and the landlady goes to some trouble to add a touch of colour with hanging baskets.

As befits a pub of that age, there have been several reports of unexplained happenings. Landlords have reported creaking floorboards, sudden patches of cold and an atmosphere that sets dogs barking.

But for locals, there is another, far stranger reason for singling out the pub for attention.

According to a legend handed down from generation to generation, in the 19th century, a few men were drinking in the pub. A brawl broke out and tankards were flung to the ground, their contents splashing over the dirty floor. One man's daughter was outside, playing in the churchyard with some of her friends when they heard the sound of the fight.

Realising that things were getting out of hand, she rushed to peer in through the small window panes, and saw her father being slain, right before her very eyes.

Her hand instinctively pressed against the glass pane, as she screamed hysterically for the murderer to stop. But it was too late. Her father was dead, and all that remained was the sweaty, desperate hand print on the glass.

According to successive landlords, the imprint has been appearing for over 200 years. Some of them thought it was a prank of some sort; others thought it was a bit of a novelty. Many of them have tried to wipe it away, polishing furiously away on first one and then the other side of the glass. In desperation, others have replaced the glass pane, but the hand-print just reappears every few months or so.

The image lasts for three to four days, resisting all efforts by patrons to breathe on it and wipe it away with the edge of a sleeve. Others place their own palms on the imprint, trying to figure out what type of person could have left it.

The window overlooks a small churchyard, and the ground on that side of the building is slightly higher than the road-level, so that the hand imprint is at roughly waist height from the outside.

George, who now lives in Malta, had been going to the Royal Stag for years. He would often just pop in there with his mates for a pint or two on his way home. For 15 years, he had never seen anything strange himself, although he had heard all about the story.

And then one day, about five years ago, he went into the pub on the way back from the Guy Fawke's festivities. It was there behind him, the imprint of a slightly damp hand on glass.

He knew that sort of imprint well; it was the sort you leave on the coffee-table that your mum always tells you off about.

Although he knew from all the stories he'd heard that the image could not be removed, he and his mates were drawn to it, anxious to touch it for themselves and see that it was not just a huge hoax.

As soon as he got home, George shook his wife awake to tell her about the ghostly image, but she was too busy to go the next day. By the time she did get around to the pub, the imprint had already started to fade, but she could still see the fingerprints quite clearly, their tips all that was left of the palm print.

The image had completely faded away by the next day, but as the landlady would tell you, it would be back…

*****

Alexia and her friend were enjoying a quick swim in Marsalforn Bay, just a few years ago. It was around two in the afternoon, on a normal summer day. The two swam out to the northern part of the bay, treading water and chatting.

It was perfectly normal till then, except that all of a sudden, all the buildings which line that side of the shore disappeared. The two friends could see only the fields that must once have covered the whole bay area. The amazed girls had enough time to look at each other and verify that they could both see the same illusion. The whole episode only lasted 30 seconds at most. Then the buildings re-appeared, gradually taking form again through the heat haze.

Double Exposure

A 15-year-old girl had no way of knowing that her holiday snaps would capture a different era.

Jackie had really looked forward to her holiday

in England. She knew the family she was going to stay with, friends of her parents, and had written to their daughter, Wendy, planning all the things they would do.

But you know what it is like with grown-ups. They have very clear ideas about what 15-year-olds are interested in, and if Jackie groaned inwardly, at least she did not say anything to offend them. She was taken around all the "interesting sites", castles, and picturesque villages, historic pubs and railway museums...

But this particular day seemed never-ending. Jackie could hardly remember the names and details of the many "tourist sites" they had been to that day. She only had a vague idea of where they were. "Somewhere near Gloucester...." The fact that there was a constant drizzle did not help. She wished they would go home.

And yet, there was something about this old village common, somewhere near the Welsh border. Something was not quite right. Jackie kept turning around, sure that Wendy was tapping her on the shoulder. But every time she turned round there was no-one there. She felt a cold shiver run down her spine.

She couldn't explain the feeling. It was not evil in any way; she tried to find the word... intense. That was it; the place felt intense.

Trying to shrug it off, she dutifully listened to Wendy's mother explain how the building had once burnt down, but really wasn't paying much attention... And then Wendy's mother looked expectantly at Jackie. Perhaps she should signify her enthusiasm for the place by taking a picture. She pulled her little Agfa camera out of her bag. It was one of those snap-open type. "Even you can't fail with one of these," her dad had laughed as he gave it to her before she left.

She took the photograph, hoping that she had managed to get the full common into the picture, and they all walked forward.

And then Jackie was overwhelmed by a strange feeling. She somehow knew that she had to take the photo again. Without pausing to think or even check the camera, she pointed and clicked. The feeling ebbed away.

The rest of her two weeks passed without further incident and she went back to Malta. Five films were duly sent in for development and one afternoon, she sat down and started slipping them into pocket albums.

"Where's this?" "Oh, look how sweet!" "Didn't it ever stop raining!?" Her family pored over the photos, making the standard comments expected of holiday snaps.

It was Jacky's elder sister who hesitated over the photos of the common. She flipped back and forth between the two photos.

"Hey," she said hesitantly. "Look at this."

Both photos had been developed. But the second photo was terrible. Her thumb obscured the bottom right-hand corner, and they seemed to have messed up the development - there was a light smudge across the front of the photo.

Jackie looked up: "I know, I guess I should throw that one away. It's not very good. Anyway, the first one came out all right."

"No," her sister managed to croak. "Look. They're different."

She took the photos out of the plastic wallet and

moved under the window. The family followed her, peering over her shoulder.

In the light, the light-coloured image at the front of the photo was quite distinctly that of a woman. Her straw-boater could be made out, and the flowing dress, cut under her bosom, had a deep frill along the bottom. She seemed to be holding a parasol behind her, and to be pushing something, perhaps a pram.

"Perhaps it is a double exposure," Jackie suggested, unconvinced, remembering with a cold shiver the feeling she had had when she took the photograph.

"No, you still haven't seen it, have you?" Her sister said, pointing at the picture. "The tree..."

In the second photo, there was a huge tree in the corner of the common which had been replaced by a huge pole in the first picture.

And unlike the image of the woman, this was crystal clear. So was a balcony on the facing building, which had been removed in the first picture, leaving a clear mark on the side of the building. The eaves on the building running along the left of the photo were also noticeably different. Each time they scrutinised the photo, they seemed to notice some other difference.

The family looked at the two photos in silence. Jackie shuddered. She wanted to destroy them, but her sister stopped her. "This is so weird..."

They looked at the negatives, thinking that these might provide some clue, but even when they took re-prints, the second photo bore the same ghostly image and the common at a different era. They wrote to the family in England, enclosing copies of the photos. They were amazed but were not able to find out any more about the common.

For nine years, Jackie kept the photos carefully locked away, only mentioning them to one or two friends. She once showed them to a keen photographer friend of hers, who was convinced that the negatives could not have been tampered with. There seemed to be no rational explanation. Eventually, reluctantly, Jackie began to accept the unthinkable. Her camera had somehow captured a photographic image of the past... or the future.

Whenever she talked about the photos, she felt that she was resurrecting the ghost, that the mysterious girl was somehow still present. And even if the feeling was reassuring rather than evil, she felt it was a force she could not understand. She was afraid of it. So she said nothing.

But now, she has told her story. And there are the photos to prove it.

One of the obvious differences is the smudge at the foreground, which is shaped like a woman. Computer-enhancing helped to define two other images in front of the central figure, which may be two children.

Some of the other inexplicable differences between the photographs:

- The tree is missing and there are now buildings in the background.
- The bricks clearly show the trace of where there was previously a balcony
- The eaves underneath the building are different
- The figures are not clear enough to make out their clothing-style, the only clue which could help to identify the era captured by the photo.

• The clock shows two different times, even though there were only seconds between one photo and the next.

Over the past nine years, the negatives have been misplaced, which unfortunately makes it very difficult to verify the authenticity of the photographs.

Pierre Stafrace, an award-winning photographer, was one of the team behind the recent adverts which, for example, showed the prehistoric temples spelling out the word "Cisk", created by manipulating photographic images with a computer.

He commented: "With computers nowadays you can do anything to a photograph, as the advert shows. The temples looked so realistic that some people asked me whether the temples really were that shape! Without looking at Jackie's negatives, it would be hard to say how possible it is that they are fakes."

And yet, why would Jackie have gone to all that trouble? For monetary gain? She has not sold them to any magazine. Just as a hoax? For nine years, she has refused to tell her story or to let else anyone pass it on on her behalf.

The photographic paper and format tallies with the date that they were supposed to been taken.

At the end of the day, it is up to the reader to decide whether he or she believes in the photographs. It is easier for me. I have met Jackie and seen the original photographs. I know the friends of hers who heard the story years ago. I saw her shudder as she told her tale.

But if you believe that the photographs are genuine, you also have to accept that there really are some things which just cannot be explained...

Castle Duty

When Tina's parents went to Scotland in August 1995, it was only natural that her Scottish father would go back to visit the places he had known as a child.

One place in particular remained in James' memory, draped in the romantic notions of youth. Gight Castle was deep in the forests, far from anywhere. The castle, originally the family seat of the Gordons, was surrounded by fields, with cattle thoughtfully munching the grass and hardly any habitation to be seen.

When his wife, Lucy, got to the edge of the field, she shook her head: had they really trudged all that way to see this pile of ruins? The walls had mostly collapsed and most of the top floor had no ceiling left.

But it fitted in with the bleak Scottish landscape and she could well imagine it in its heyday, around four hundred years before. Still she was not surprised that they were the only people around.

When they got to the castle, James remembered his way around in that curious way in which childhood memories can resurface. Lucy wandered off to one side and he went up to the top floor. Tina was awed by it all. Just seven-years-old, she was a voracious reader and knew all about castles and things. She made her way gingerly up the spiral staircase, which had no balustrades, keeping as close to the wall as she could. She found herself on the roof with ramparts overlooking the fields below. She picked her way over the fallen stones, following her father.

At one point on the wall, there was a small enclosure. She figured that it had probably been used by the guards to shoot from. But as she stood there day-dreaming, she was quite taken aback to see someone walk past the entrance, and continue along the wall. She turned to her dad, who was looking out over the wall a short distance away from her, and asked: "Dad! Who was that? That man in the top hat...?"

James looked round in surprise, but when they looked back, there was no-one there. There was nowhere anyone could have gone either. Tina described the man: he had his face turned away from her, but he was wearing a very dark blue top hat.

Tina herself began to wonder whether she was seeing things, and her father played down the incident, not wanting to frighten her. But as they continued working their way round the ruins, he looked out of a window cut into the wall of one of the staircases and noticed a wing of the castle that he had never seen before.

He checked his bearings but was convinced that he had never noticed it.

He walked down the stairs and worked his way to where the wing should be, but when he got there, there was only a gable-end and no sign on the ground of any foundations. Perhaps he had lost his way. He made his way back to the window, and looked out again, but the wing had disappeared. He shook himself. What could he do but doubt his own senses?

When they got back to the village, James went to look up his old scout-master. Tina was bursting to tell someone about the man she had seen, convinced that it was a ghost.

Perhaps it had been...

The scoutmaster told them that there had been two tragedies connected to the history of the castle. Apparently, the owner's daughter had fallen in love with a tailor he considered to be unworthy of her. The besotted tailor sneaked into the castle disguised as one of the bagpipers, and later that night eloped with the girl. The owner of the castle gave chase and apparently the couple were killed.

The other tragedy took place some time later. The lord of the castle was riding past a well, when a young maid stood up carrying her pails of water. The sudden movement frightened the horse who reared up, throwing the lord to the ground. He was killed on the spot.

Neither story would have accounted for the family's strange experience. Had they really seen something strange at the castle? The scoutmaster did not remember hearing any stories but then again, children are very open, very believing.

Tina saw something, even though she herself still wonders what it might have been.

"He was real, I mean I could not see through him or anything I suppose he was a *bit* faint," she said, as she scribbled a little map to show where she had been, and where her father had been, and how the field was full of cows..

"And he was wearing a strange, tall, blue top hat..."

At The Top Of The Stairs

There is something about a *garigor* that plays on a child's imagination. The twists and turns of the stairs create deep pools of shadows, and disembodied voices seem to carry up the stairwell.

And Marianne shared a room with her sister half-way up the winding stairs. So perhaps it was no surprise that she used to lie in bed with the covers pulled up high, occasionally glancing across at her sister in the next bed. She often wished she had the courage to jump out of bed and in with her sister, but she knew that Daniella, six years her senior, would tease her for being a real baby. And seven was too old to be such a baby, wasn't it?

But she was so frightened of the footsteps. At least once a week, for years on end, she would hear them. They seemed to start way down below from the most terrifying place in the house, *taht it-tarag*, the little, triangular cubby-hole at the foot of the stairs that was not really big enough for anything but the odd box and tin, and yet seemed large enough for all a child's nightmares and fears.

There were two pairs of footsteps, and she could visualise the people as they came up, one slightly ahead of the other on the narrow stairs.

And then they would come to the landing. And Marianne would see them. They would turn and stand silently side-by-side in her doorway, an elderly couple, the man dressed in a dark, formal suit, the lady in a black dress. Neither of them had their heads covered.

Marianne would try to lie as still as possible. "Perhaps if I don't move," she thought, with the innocence of youth, "they'll think I'm dead."

They would stare intently at the two lying figures and after a few seconds they would turn and disappear again, leaving the little child shaking in her bed.

She would close her eyes tightly and then start

yelling at the top of her voice. "Ma, ma!" And her mother would come and calm her down, trying to stop her from waking up her sister nearby. She always had the same explanation: "It's probably just the neighbours you can hear..." Although her mother never said so in as many words, Marianne was sure she thought that the whole thing was just an over-active imagination.

And over the years, she too began to wonder. She moved in to a bigger room when she was 10 and never saw or heard anything again. Yet she would dread having to go up the *garigor* and would go to all sorts of lengths to avoid it. There were times she could not get out of it, though, like when her father wanted her to fetch something. Then she would take a deep breath and run all the way up and all the way down without stopping to even look into her old bedroom. But children do grow up and she did begin to feel silly. After all, her brother had slept in that room before her and he had never complained about seeing or hearing anything.

With time, she forgot all about the strange couple, peering at her through the dark.

Until she read one of the "Unexplained" stories in a *Weekender* and brought up the subject over their family get-together. They discussed the story that had appeared in that issue and then, with a bit of a laugh, Marianne turned to her mother and said: "Remember when I was little and I used to see that old couple standing on the stairs?" Her mother nodded, smiling.

But Marianne's sister, Daniella, did not.

"I never told you," she said to Marianne. "I didn't want to frighten you, but I used to hear them and see them too. And perhaps because I was older, I never called out for mum or anything. But, yes. I used to see them every week too."

A hush fell over the dinner table. And Marianne felt a cold shiver run up her spine.

****

Marianne's is not the only story told by a child. Anna remembers when she was a young girl, playing outside in the street in Pieta with her friends. It was different in the early '50s: no television, few cars. They played near a fountain alongside the old cemetery where plague victims were buried. It's no use trying to find it. There is a big block of flats there now.

But Anna once saw a frail, little boy, dressed in his Holy Communion outfit, peering at them through the glass *antiporta* of the house at the side of the road. He looked so lonely, so forlorn that she thought of beckoning to him to come out and play with them. And yet, she knew the family that lived there. They had no children and she had never seen the little boy before.

She did not have much time to think about it, because by the time she looked round again, the white-clad figure had disappeared.

She asked her mother and neighbours whether they had seen a little boy. No-one had. But to this day, Anna is sure that she saw the lonely spirit of a young boy, enviously watching the playing children.

****

A family were renting a flat which had a piano. Their young daughter used to sit and play and complain that someone was pushing her to the side on the stool as if to move her out of the way. When they moved out, the owner said that she was so glad the piano had been used as her father used to love to sit next to her and play...

Another piano story involved a woman who went to baby-sit her sister's children. She was quite pleased when they went to bed without any fuss, and she stayed up to watch some television. The whole house was quiet by the time she went to bed after the 11 o'clock news. So she thought it rather odd that one of the children would get up to play the piano in the middle of the night. She got up to investigate, padding downstairs in her slippers to find the sitting-room in total darkness. She fumbled for the light switch and turned it on. The music stopped suddenly. There was no-one in the room. The children were all still fast asleep in their beds.

****

The new secretary had to work long hours. It was a new company and there was lots to do. One evening her boss was away, and she was struggling to cope. Already stressed, the last thing she needed was to have to look for the inkpad and stamp. They were nowhere to be found. Days later, she went upstairs to the store-room to look for something, and found the inkpad lying up there. She had not been up there for days.

A little while later her ruler disappeared and it too turned up in the store-room. The most inexplicable thing though was a filing cabinet, which had been moved a few feet out from the wall. No-one else had been in the building except the cleaner, who took one look at the heavy cabinet and scoffed. "As if I could move that heavy thing, even if I wanted to..." Although the secretary never saw anything, she is sure that when she went upstairs, she felt pressure on her back as though someone was urging her upstairs, The building was often filled with strange, unaccountable noises. The building had been empty for 15 years before they moved in. She wonders why?

****

One night Josette woke up to find her bedside radio was on. That in itself would have been strange enough, but it was playing classical music on an Italian station that she had never tuned in to before. Her first thought was that there had been a power cut, but the clock was not flashing as it would have been. Perplexed, she went back to sleep.

The next day, she found out that her favourite uncle had died, the one that used to love listening to Italian classical music...

Religious Relic

It has been almost 50 years, but Joseph still remembers his unexplained encounter

Joseph was always a dedicated worker. He was never one to leave work unfinished, and so it was not unusual for him to go into work one Sunday morning. It is such a quiet time, no people, no interruptions, no phone calls. He was looking forward to getting a lot of work done.

The office was in a big spacious building in Valletta, with a huge staircase winding up through the centre of it. He carefully shut and bolted the big door behind him and walked up to the top floor.

He settled down to his work, relishing the peace and quiet.

Perhaps this is why he was so perturbed to hear footsteps. The interruption was certainly not welcome. He idly wondered who it was, and tried to concentrate on his work again, but the sound of the footsteps going downstairs persisted in his subconscious. With a little sigh, he stood up and went to the banisters to see who had decided to put in a little overtime.

Below him, his habit swaying as he walked, was a Franciscan friar.

Joseph watched him work his way to the bottom without too much alarm, thinking that he must have come in with another colleague. The friar turned out of sight and the echoing steps gradually gave way to silence.

But the thought nagged him that he had not heard the heavy door open or close, and if he had been let in by anyone else, there was certainly no trace of them. He decided to investigate, checking that all the offices were closed and empty. He worked his way down the building, until he finally had to admit to himself that there was no-one there. The main door remained shut and bolted and yet there was no trace of the priest whatsoever. Joseph shrugged off the incident, returned to his work upstairs and forgot all about it.

Some time later, the company moved offices and he was chatting to his fiancee who worked in the accounts department. They were talking about the move and one of the other girls in the office threw in a casual remark.

"At least we won't get that priest coming in any more…"

Joseph's ears pricked up. "What priest?"

"Oh, he was so rude. *X'wicc tost*! This Franciscan friar, he used to come through the office to go to the toilet, and you know he never even asked. He just used to walk straight through the office and out again without ever saying word."

The other girls nodded in agreement.

Was it related? Was the monk a ghostly visitor to the offices that they had just assumed was a real person?

The house was originally a private house, built at the end of the 17th century. It was eventually passed on from the Pitardi family that owned it and for some time was used as the Hospital for Incurable Women. Over the years since then, the building has changed hands many times and is now owned by a couple who have an 11-year-old son. The woman is terribly sceptical about the story but she admits that she has often wondered… When her son was just three-years-old, he came in screaming that he had seen a green-faced person.

But her mother has often said she could not understand how they could possibly live there. Over the past years, she has stubbornly refused to sleep over, claiming that the house is full of strange, unexplained noises. The occupier is not convinced; she has never heard or seen anything.

Still, she has never been able to come up with an explanation for the things which keep disappearing from her son's room, which never, ever seem to turn up again.

****

The 50-year old woman woke up, startled by the noise from outside. She went to the window to investigate, peeping through the curtains expecting to see daylight. But it was still dark, cold... Down the narrow street, a funeral procession was wending its way. The hearse was being drawn by horses, the noises of their hooves echoing down the road. The hearse itself was covered in wreaths, and there were sombrely dressed mourners following on foot. She watched in silence, thinking that it must have been someone terribly important to have such an impressive funeral, wondering where the horses had come from. The procession worked its way slowly down the street and disappeared around the corner.

The street was quiet again, and the woman let the curtain fall back. She picked up her clock: it was four in the morning. But the thought suddenly occurred to her: no-one can be buried before dawn. In the newspapers that day, no deaths were reported. There had been no funerals.

War Story

By May, 1943, Albert Crockford – Bert to all who knew him – had already seen more of the war than he could ever have wanted to. And he was still just 23. He had lived through Dunkirk and been wounded at El Alamein. He considered himself to be quite a tough little fellow really, not easily scared. And the three corporals he was bunked down with had their own horror stories. No, they were a tough bunch all right.

Just released from one hospital, Bert found himself posted to yet another, just on the outskirts of

Alexandria, but this time it was quite different. The imposing Victorian buildings had once served as a school for wealthy Egyptian children, and had been converted for temporary use as a military hospital.

Bert and his pals, Biggy, Neville and Joe, would have been pleased to be anywhere in the imposing building with its vast, landscaped gardens, but they were especially pleased by their room. It was one of two built into the corners of the flat-roofed building. It was cool up there, a breeze constantly wafting through the three, airy windows. And it was quiet, too.

In the past, the rooms had been used for storage by the teachers and there was still one relic of those days: a huge, heavy, wooden box with a hinged lid. This box sat outside the window by Bert's bed and the men used it as a seat for the odd cigarette before they went to sleep. It also made a convenient dust-bin, although they had been forced to put a card-board box inside it so it could be emptied out more easily.

All it all, it was not a bad life, considering that the war was still raging. But on May 28, something happened...

The men were all propped up on their beds at around 11pm, having a last chat and cigarette before turning in for the night, when they heard the box being dragged away. "Some bugger's trying to steal our box!" they yelled, and ran to the door of their room.

It was a clear, moonlit night. They could see all the way across the roof to the other hut and the top of the lit staircase. And there was no-one there.

But the box had been pulled five feet away from the wall.

The four did not quite know what to do. There was clearly no-one around, and eventually they decided to go back to bed, assuming that if it was a prankster, he'd be back. They chatted for a while, ruling out the possibility that the wind had blown the box – it would have taken a hurricane to move that box! There didn't seem to be many other plausible explanations and they soon fell silent.

The minutes seemed to tick away in slow-motion. Without saying a word to each other, all four realised that something else was going to happen. Twenty minutes had passed by, and the men were just beginning to doze off when the noise started up again, a relentless, scraping noise.

This time, the men wasted no time. Rather than run to the door, they leapt up onto Bert's bed and peered anxiously out of the window. There was nothing. And yet the box was this time even further away, closer to the parapet wall.

The men searched everywhere, knowing how futile it was even as they did so. After all, there was nowhere for anyone to be concealed, not even any shadows for the 'person' to hide in. Still, they looked wherever they could, even on the roof of their room. Nothing.

Then one of them mentioned that it was getting close to midnight. Terrific. Now they were *all* terrified out of their wits! They shut the door and found some excuse to leave the lights on. And then they waited, deadly sure that something was about to happen.

This time, they did not have to wait long. The box again started its journey, scraping and grating against the rough floor-tiles. The men sat bolt upright, hardly able to breathe, the hairs on the back of their necks bristling uncomfortably.

The dragging seemed to last an eternity. But they suddenly heard a gentle thump as the box hit the edge of the parapet, and there was then a deafening silence. It did not last long, however. It was soon pierced by a hideous scream, a hysterical laugh, and then silence once again. The scream had come from outside the far window; below it there was only a 50 foot drop down to the ground.

Bert and the others thought that the prankster must have fallen over the edge of the wall, even though the parapet was at least four foot high. They snapped out of the trance that they had fallen into while listening to the box and ran outside. There was still nobody around but the box was now further away, up against the wall. It looked perfectly normal, and yet they shuddered, an icy finger running up their spines.

They steeled themselves to look over, sure that they would see a broken body three storeys below. Bert could not even begin to express their relief when they realised that there was nothing there. The sound of that horrifying scream still rang in their ears and yet no curious lights were switched on below. The hospital slumbered peacefully.

It was a long night, the men haunted by the unexplainable noise and that...

They didn't even want to think about it.

The days passed and no-one at the hospital mentioned any strange noises. The men gradually forgot about it. Until a few weeks later.

Bert had gone down to the hospital laundry to collect his uniform and he got into a conversation with one of the Arabs who worked there. He was a pleasant fellow and Bert was impressed by his

English. The Egyptian mentioned that his father used to work as a gardener for the school when he was still a young boy. Thinking of the lush, beautiful gardens, Bert mentioned casually that it must have been a pleasant place to work.

And the Egyptian agreed, adding that not everyone thought so, though. He said he remembered that his father had come home once, rather excited with some terrible news. It seemed that the previous night, one of the teachers had dragged a table or something from the roof hut to the edge of the parapet and leapt to his death.

Bert could get no more information out of the man. The Egyptian had only been a little boy when his father had told him the story, and his father had since died. And yet, Bert felt the cold shiver brush down his spine once again as he realised that he would now never be able to forget that dreadful, scraping noise.

Bert Crockford, then 76, lived in Malta. He kept careful notes of his experiences during the war, which he has since compiled into a fascinating diary.

Forecast

Can an event have an 'echo' before it happens?

Roberta was curled up on the sofa, a blanket over her feet to keep them warm. She took a sip from her mug of hot chocolate.

She had seen the film before, but was enjoying it even more the second time around. She was so engrossed that she hardly noticed the scraping of the key in the front door but her conscience pricked her. With one last glance at the TV screen, she pulled the cover off her feet and turned round.

"Mario? Did you have a nice time?"

Her elder brother was allowed to stay out much later than she was, even though she was already in her 20s. She knew that boys were always treated a bit differently anyway. But he had the added bonus of having a fiancée, which meant he could stay out till 10 p.m. without any questions being asked.

When he didn't answer, she got up, her toes curling up against the cold floor, and padded into the kitchen for a bit of a chat. Perhaps he would watch the end of the film with her.

But the room was still dark and silent. There was no-one there.

Roberta stood there for a moment, a bit confused. She had heard the lock, then the door. But if it wasn't Mario, then who?

She returned to her film, but somehow it had lost its appeal. She soon decided to go to bed, but as she was walking upstairs, the key turned once again in the lock. She stopped, frozen. Every nerve in her body tingled, her eyed glued to the door. Her heart almost stopped when the door handle turned and the door creaked open.

She almost let out a sob of relief when the familiar figure of her brother walked into the hallway.

She was so overcome with the cold chill of relief that she could hardly tell him what had happened. It seemed so foolish once he was actually standing there in the house.

She would probably have forgotten all about it, except for the fact that the same thing happened again. And again. And she was not the only person who heard the door open.

One evening, Mario was once again out with his

fiancée. Roberta was already up in her room, her younger brother Nicholas was fast asleep, and her parents were probably asleep. But her father heard the key turn in the lock and the door open and slam shut. The light went on in the hall below, throwing grotesque shadows up the stairs and across their doorways. The dog sleeping at the end of the bed stirred. Her ears pricked up and she leapt off the bed, and slunk down low, her tail flat behind her. She crept to the top of the stairs and growled menacingly.

But there was no-one there. Each of them tried to laugh it off. Roberta suggested as cheerfully as she could that Mario must have come home but changed his mind and gone out again. Perhaps, she tried to persuade herself, he only came in to pick something off the hat-stand, like a jacket. Maybe he was feeling cold. Yes, that must have been it.

But when he did come home about a quarter of an hour later, he was surprised to see them all still up. He had not been anywhere near the house when they had heard the door open.

It was down to Roberta's father to find a solution to this intriguing mystery. He struck on the perfect one. It must have been their neighbour. Perhaps he had came home a bit worse for wear and came into their house instead of his own.

Roberta did not have the heart to point out that the chances of his key being able to open their door was probably very remote...

There is no end to this story. The family still lives in Birkirkara on a fairly busy road. The strange 'pre-echo' of Mario coming home did not occur again, but the family never did find any rational explanation

Valletta Visitor

Francesca was not what you would call the worrying kind. A foreigner married to a Maltese, she brooded over her three children like a mother hen, practical and too busy to allow her imagination to get the better of her.

She was therefore awake but not fretting when it had turned 2 a.m. on a Sunday morning. There was still no sign of her eldest daughter, who had been out to a wedding and then to savour the nightlife in Paceville. She stood shivering behind the cold glass panes of the bedroom window, listening to the wild wind, which always seemed to whistle down the road.

Litter and other papers swirled around in the wind eddies, but then Francesca noticed another movement. Out of the corner of her eye, against the walls of an 18th century building, a man was standing alone. She could swear that he had not walked down the street, but there he suddenly was, dressed in a dark cape and a top hat. He started pacing in front of the building's main door.

Francesca felt even colder. There was something unnatural about the man, dressed so strangely, pacing up and down at that time of night. And he was so tall. Far taller than anyone else she knew. As she watched, he lifted off the ground and floated gently up as high as the first floor before gradually thinning out and disappearing completely. Poor Francesca watched in horror.

Just then a car pulled up in the road and stopped to deliver her daughter. The whispers and the giggles and the slam of the car door echoed down the deserted road. Francesca had to tell someone although she was worried about being met with scepticism. To her surprise, her sister-in-law Pauline who lived nearby, lowered her voice, and holding onto her arm, said: "I've never seen anything myself, but I know plenty of others who have."

Months passed and Pauline's son had his foreign fiancee over in Malta on holiday. Coming home at around 2.30 a.m., he dropped Sharon off outside the house, and drove around the block to try and find a parking place. As she waited for him on the doorstep, she noticed a tall, dark figure standing outside the *palazzo*. She gave him a second glance because of his size and his strange clothes, but then turned away. However, when she next looked around, he rose into the air and disappeared.

Sharon eventually told Pauline. But still, Francesca was not one to fret. She was too pragmatic to worry about the man. She was just reassured that she had not been imagining things.

This is not the only story about the caped man. About 30 years ago, Fred was considered to be a fancy dresser. He worked in one of the bars in Strait Street, when it was a busy, rollicking area, and would come home very late at night, dressed in really smart suits, draped in gold chains, and rings, and carrying most of the day's takings.

His sister, Carmelina, was always telling him off, worried that he would one day be mugged. But he would smile secretly and reassure her: "My friend accompanies me home," he said enigmatically. "No one would dare touch me when he is there."

He described his friend as being extremely tall and said he usually wore a dark cape. He would walk to the corner and when they reached the *palazzo*, they nodded at each other in silence and the man would vanish. This happened every night, year in, year out. Fred was never mugged. He never let on who the caped crusader was...

The Caped Man seems to favour late night sightings by anxious relatives. Last summer, Angela, who lives a few hundred yards from the *palazzo*, along another street, was also waiting for her daughter to return. It was hot and sticky, and she went out on to the balcony. She spotted the man lingering outside. She hesitated for a while, then went back inside, pulling the *persjani* behind her.

As she fastened the latch, leaving them ajar, she suddenly heard a large fluttering noise. It was as though dozens of giant butterflies were beating their wings against the walls. She quickly opened the shutters again, only to see the man literally fading away.

The *palazzo* is now used as a school, and until recently a woman was hired to look after the premises after hours. One day a few years ago, just as she was locking up after school, a couple of students went up to Rita. They had forgotten some books in the classroom. Could they just go and fetch them? She let them in and they disappeared into the courtyard, only to return a few moments later.

"Don't lock up yet, there is still someone here," they told her.

"Don't be stupid," she said. " Why would anyone want to stay here after school?"

But she went up with them and there was indeed a man, up at the first floor window. He stared at them and turned away into the darkness.

They didn't stop to check who he was. The three of them just turned tail and ran.

These are just a few of the many stories about

the palazzo. There are many others, which could not be verified because they happened long ago, or to people who have since moved from this street. But there are too many to ignore. Who can be sure how many others have seen the Caped Man but just thought he was a strange sight?

CHAPTER THREE

It would be naïve to think that ghosts are all benevolent. Some are mischievous, others verge on cruel. Some of them are malicious enough to drive people out of their homes. Imagine giving up a family home, moving away from neighbours and friends, selling up at a loss... It is not a decision to be taken lightly.

This fact, more than many others, is proof of just how deeply those I interviewed believed that they were being haunted.

Catherine looked at Gianni's watch. It was almost 10.30 p.m. They were engaged, but in spite of this and the fact that she was already in her 20s, she still had to be home by a certain time. Gianni hated it.

But time it was. They had been courting in the shadows, down a little lane and, still whispering sweet nothings to each other, they walked slowly down the lane to the main road, lingering as long as possible.

There is now a garden and a housing estate on the main road which leads into Zabbar, but then it used to be an open piece of ground with a rubble wall round the perimeter, Gianni and his pals often played football there, but his thoughts were miles away from sport.

As they went round the corner, they came abruptly into a pool of light from the street lamp. Before their eyes had properly adjusted, Gianni gave a startled cry and grabbed Catherine's arm even tighter. Leaning back against the wall was a man, wearing a long, dark cloak, his face hidden in its shadows. He swears that the man was much taller than normal, almost seven feet tall, but it was not that which had caused him to pull away. The man had an aura of threat, almost of evil.

Catherine ignored him, wanting to get home before her dad noticed how late she was. But Gianni refused to pass by the stranger, pulling her over to the other side of the road. As they walked down the road, the only sound was the tap-tapping of Catherine's heels. Gianni looked back anxiously over his shoulder but the man still stood there, not moving, in the pool of light.

Gianni felt rather silly about it. Looking back on it in the cold light of day, so to speak, he could not explain why he had felt threatened.

Till four days later. He was at the band club playing billiards with a friend, when Reno pulled him over to a quieter part of the room.

"Gianni, you'll never believe this," he started. "You know the field, the one where we play football? Well, a few days ago, I was walking Grace home and we were, you know, holding hands. And then I saw this man coming up towards us, and, I don't know why, but I felt really frightened of him. I suppose it was because I couldn't see his face, because he was wearing some sort of long cloak. Anyway, he just pushed straight between us. I shivered, I can tell you that. I felt frozen where he had brushed against me..."

It had been the same day, the same place, Zabbar in 1951.

Seven years later, a company was drilling by the bastions there. One night a power cut plunged the engineers into darkness. One of them, a Scottish guy, was sent out to investigate. He walked up to the wall that ran along the side of the bastions, checking the cable connections that they had put there temporarily while they were drilling. Everything seemed to be fine. But his message did not get back to the other engineers, who were still waiting in candlelight for the electricity to be switched on again.

When a few hours had passed, another man was sent out to look for him. He was found unconscious by the wall. When they managed to revive him, he said that a tall man, wearing a dark cloak, had just picked him up like a ragdoll and thrown him against the wall.

These three 'sightings' of a tall, cloaked man, would qualify for the title of strange all on their own.

But years later, Gianni found a book in a jumble sale in Canada. In it there was the story of an Englishman, Humphrey Saunders, who died in mysterious circumstances in the Verdala barracks in 1935.

"*Across the square, he could see a remarkably tall man in a long, dark cloak, standing motionless under one of the mess windows. Something about the appearance of this solitary shrouded figure attracted his attention. To be wearing such clothes in a Mediterranean heatwave seemed peculiar.*

With a leap, the cloaked man sprang onto the windowsill and disappeared through the curtains into the mess... Then after a few seconds, an ear-piercing scream rang out - a harsh, appalling cry of rage and terror, and to his horror and utter amazement, he saw the man reappear at the window with Saunders in his arms. Both men vanished around the corner...

He ran to the mess and found the card-room in chaos. On the floor, surrounded by half a dozen officers, lay Saunders, dead.

A formal military enquiry revealed that no civilian was in the garrison after 10 p.m. that day.

The card-players testified in their evidence that a momentary gust of wind seemed to shake the nearest window. Simultaneously, the card table was stirred, and Saunders, throwing his hands up into the air, slumped in his chair gasping as though in a fit. Medical evidence showed that he had died of a heart attack..."

(*Strange Destinies*, by Jon Macklin, published by ACE)

Midnight Mischief

Although Philip and Sheila had a lovely house in Rabat, they knew it wasn't The Right One. It was 1976, they were not married yet, but they and a group of friends all "hung" out together, living in a sort of commune arrangement.

As is often the case when looking for something, you come across it in the most unexpected way.

Philip and Sheila went to see literally dozens of houses from various real-estate agents, but all were discarded without a second thought. But there was one old farmhouse in one of the Three Villages that they immediately fell in love with. The house was 500 years old in parts and boasted 22 rooms.

Unfortunately, it also cost twice their budget. The disappointed pair listened to the door click shut as the agent showed them back to the car, but a little bit of the house's atmosphere seemed to leave with them.

Philip was determined to have the house, one way or another. He felt that if he could just speak to the owner in person, he could somehow persuade him to sell it.

For two years, he searched through the land registry files and pestered neighbours, but he could not track down the owner. Then one day, an English friend of theirs, Kerry, came down to stay with them for a holiday.

They did all the usual sights and then for no particular reason, drove her to the end of the alley to show her their "dream house" or at least all they could see of it: the locked door.

Was it fate? She immediately said: "Oh, I know the owner". And so it was. He was coming to Malta just a few days later. Philip went down to meet him, he pleaded his case and was perhaps the most surprised of all when it worked. The owner halved the price and gave him the key there and then.

The couple and their three friends moved in almost immediately. Life got into a routine quickly - they went to work, came home and ate together, played guitars and talked. But then their lives started to be manipulated in ways they could not at first understand, let alone believe.

At first the incidents were minor and easily explained away as carelessness, or the consequence of too many people sharing one house. Keys hung up carefully on a hook would turn up in a bedroom.

A wallet would be found underneath the bed, in the wrong person's room. But nothing actually disappeared. The normally placid dog would go mad, growling and snarling by one particular corner, but gradually learnt to avoid it.

Life continued.

Till one day, the five were sitting watching television, when they heard clapping from upstairs. Just that, two or three claps, and then nothing. They did a quick head-count to check that no one had gone upstairs, and then turned off the television. But there was just a thick, heavy silence.

With a little nervous chuckle, the television was switched on again. But this time, Philip watched the bottom of the stairs out of the corner of his eye. Clap. Clap. This time, the lights in the hallway went on and off with the sound.

An explanation: it was just an electrical fault. Philip and one of the men decided to go and investigate. They only got as far as the bottom of the stairs. Clap. Clap. The lights flickered again, and ignoring any attempt at bravado, the two just ran back in terror.

They sat in silence for a while and as the minutes ticked away, the five suddenly felt rather foolish. The two men went to the mains and turned off the electricity, and they all sat silently, waiting in the half light of dusk. The claps echoed one more time. They looked at each other - what next?

Soon after, the friends were again terrified by noises, this time louder and more inexplicable than before. For three consecutive nights, they were awoken by screeching noises from the courtyard, like an empty metal container being dragged across the flagstones.

This time, the friends peered out of their windows to the quiet courtyard below. The scene was as peaceful as one would expect at three in the morning, and yet the awful noise continued. This time, the need to find a rational explanation made them blame the water in the pipes. But no neighbours heard the grating sounds, either on that first night or on either of the two subsequent ones. Philip remained perplexed. He examined the yard with the help of the torch, convinced that he would find gouges in the flagstones. But there was nothing, nothing at all.

But then one night, John and Michelle came down to breakfast, looking dishevelled and upset. They had obviously had a bad night. It wasn't just the lack of sleep which made them touchy either.

They had been kept awake by some prankster who kept knocking on their door and running away. The others looked at each other. Why would anyone want to do that? But John shook his head.

The prankster was not one of them. After the third or fourth bout of knocking, he had stood in wait behind the door, flinging it open as soon as the noise began again. The corridor to the right and left of their room was completely empty.

By now, Philip and Sheila and their friends were terrified. A priest was called for advice, but all he could do was reassure them that at least nothing physical had happened and they were still in no danger. The intense pace of the incidents slowed down. Weeks went by without any strange phenomena at all. Gradually their fears abated. They even started to look upon the incidents as a bit of an adventure.

But it was not all over. Philip was sitting in the living room - by now they had got a sofa and various other pieces of furniture - when he saw Sheila come down the stairs and turn into the kitchen. She was wearing a long white shift, and her light brown hair was loose.

For a moment, he was convinced that she hadn't actually opened the door.

"Shee, you couldn't get me a drink while you're in there, could you?" he called out. No reply. He got up to investigate. There was no one in the kitchen.

Sheila called out from her bedroom.

"Did you want me?"

She came down the stairs wearing a brightly coloured shirt and jeans. There was no one else around.

Sheila also had an experience. The sound of a beautiful choir suddenly filled the air. Had one of their neighbours all of a sudden developed a liking for choral music?

One evening, while walking through Paceville, Philip's attention was caught by a rather strange looking man, who was sitting on a doorstep, strumming a guitar.

He was dressed in layer upon layer of fringed garments, with long, fluffy hair, just sitting there on the ground. Philip was intrigued by his playing. They started talking and he eventually invited Scott back to the farmhouse for a barbecue that weekend.

When he arrived, about 20 of them were already in the courtyard, sitting around on cushions and mattresses. Before Philip even had a chance to introduce his new friend, Scott stopped dead in his tracks.

With eyes shut, he spread his arms out wide and started humming. His arms started moving in open circles. His friends watched in amazement, wondering who Philip had brought along.

Opening his eyes, Scott looked at Philip

"Do you know that you have got a poltergeist?" he asked.

It turned out that he was in Malta to do research for a book on phenomena and that he was the head of parapsychology at a university in South Africa, one of the best known in his field.

He was shown around the house, reacting sharply to this area or that, pausing by a wall, but always coming back to the courtyard. He was convinced that a young girl, aged in her twenties, had plunged to her death there, perhaps centuries before. The image he sensed was of a girl made pregnant by her master, who either threw herself, or was pushed, off the roof.

He quizzed Philip about the woman he had seen, the only time that any presence had actually been visible. He believed that a ghost is a sort of photograph, which also fades with time, and by describing the colour of the woman's shift decided that it had been about 250 years since she had died.

He explained the current thought that he was

outlining in his book: that when death occurs naturally the life-energy has time to dissipate gradually. But when the death is traumatic, the energy state changed too rapidly, and the energy lingered on far longer.

He also believed that the "ghostly" energy was trapped in the house, and that the reason the sightings were becoming less frequent was because Philip and his friends had changed so much in the house: doors, windows, corridors. The energy was literally getting lost.

The friends stayed on in the house for almost 12 years. Philip and Sheila got married and had kids. There were more parties, more evenings playing guitar. But there were no more sightings, and no more inexplicable phenomena.

When they look back on those months, Philip and Sheila do so with curiosity rather than fear. But they still wonder whether there was any rational explanation.

On the whole, they don't think so.

The Sins of the Past

Of course, no wife likes being left on her own. But when your husband works with the navy, there's not much you can do about it. Still, some times are worse than others.

Having just moved into a lovely house in Floriana, Jessie found that her domestic instincts were taking over. She wanted to make the house into a home and she would have liked Joseph to be there more to share it with her.

The people who sold them the house had left it in a good enough state, but there was still much to do.

So when Joseph left to go to work, sometimes for a week and a half, sometimes just for a few days, Jessie decided to spend her honeymoon pottering around.

The house seemed huge and empty at night. Alone for probably the first time in her life, Jessie was on edge. Was it her overworked imagination perhaps? Was the dark silence of the house making her feeling particularly vulnerable?

Whatever the possible psychological explanation, what happened to Jessie terrified her. She was woken up by the sound of crying. There were raised voices uttering blasphemous oaths. And there was the creaking sound of footsteps on the wooden stairs.

Jessie sat up terrified, not thinking clearly enough to realise that the flight of steps was made of stone. There was nothing she could do. Paralysed by fear, there was no way she was going to leave the bedroom to see if there was anything there.

When Joseph returned later that night, he found his wife cowering with fear in the bed. He searched the house, but of course, there was nothing there. Or was there?

The next day, Jessie found herself standing at the top of the stairs, emboldened by the daylight. The scene below her looked so peaceful and yet what demons lurked in the walls? Perhaps she was overcome by the memory of her night of terror? Perhaps, she was pushed... That's what she thinks. In any case, she found herself falling, tumbling down the stairs, luckily landing only winded.

Every night, she would hear the slow, shuffling footsteps; many times she heard the manic voice screaming and shouting.

Whatever "it" was, Jessie found herself torment-ed.

She would feel the warm breath of someone standing behind her. When she was in the bath, she would feel someone running their fingers up her spine. One morning, she was on her way out to buy bread, but the spirit had different ideas. As she went down the stairs, it gripped her by her ankles, refusing to let go.

One night, once again alone in the house, she went into the bathroom to get cleaned up before she went to sleep. As she stood at the sink, Jessie heard the door of the bathroom close. And just as clearly, she heard the key on the outside turn in the lock. She banged on the door and cried out. But who was there to hear her? It was some time before Jessie finally accepted that there was nothing she could do. No amount of crying and banging was going to get her out of the bathroom.

She spent a terrifying night locked in there, unable to sleep for fear of what she might see or hear. Dawn seemed an interminably long time away. But eventually, she heard Joseph opening the door downstairs and she almost sobbed with relief.

"Joseph," she screamed. And no sooner had she done so than the door flew open, taunting her with her helplessness over whatever possessed the house. Joseph was at a loss. He was completely sceptical and had not seen or heard anything himself. He could not believe that a simple house could terrify his wife, turning her into the person who threw her-self into his arms racked by sobs.

But he was not to be spared. One night as they were asleep in their bed, the whole bed started to shake. It was the final straw. They had only been in their first home for around three weeks, but Jessie could not bear to stay there a moment longer.

That very night, she went to stay with her inlaws, until Joseph could find them somewhere else to stay.

But Jessie was tormented by the memories of the house. Whenever she closed her eyes, she could still hear the wailing, the raised voices and the hollow footsteps on non-existent wooden stairs. She started asking about the history of the house.

The people they had bought it from claimed they had had no problems there at all, but eventually her persistence paid off. She found out that the house had once, a long time ago, been used as a mental asylum.

Who knows if the rumour were true? That in those days, the patients were locked up, tortured and tormented by their minders... perhaps even killed?

Jessie is in her 90s now and many of her memories have faded away. But she still remembers the house in Floriana. The house is still there and people are living in it. Perhaps they do not hear the tormented voices. Perhaps they do not want to. Jessie only knows that if she shuts her eyes, she still does.

Car Capers

It is always hard to find a good place to be alone with your girlfriend. But in front of a deserted chapel, out on a dark country road, surely you should be guaranteed at least a few moments of privacy?

Michael was 19-years-old, and very, very proud of his new car. He couldn't wait to take his new girlfriend out on the weekend. It was just getting dark when they drove out to the little chapel at Tal-Balal known as the Chapel of St Philip and St Jacob.

The chapel is a little gem of rural architecture, built in 1730. According to the entry in *"Bliet u Rhula Maltin"*, it has a little belfry and a single bell. The book calls it "an unexpected façade", one you would not expect to find at Tal-Balal.

And unexpected is certainly what it turned out to be for Michael, who certainly did not have architecture on his mind. In fact, for a first date, he and his girlfriend were getting on very well indeed. So much so that he needed a quick breath of fresh air, and got out of the car to answer the call of nature.

The area was deserted. Every now and then, the lights of a car would whizz past but the place would once again be plunged into inky blackness. There was no-one else around.

Michael got back into his car, and tried to get his arm round his girlfriend again, in that nonchalant way that 19-year-olds have, anxious not to rush the girl but also conscious that he had to work fast as she would have to be home soon.

But the romantic atmosphere was suddenly shattered. Someone was banging on all the windows of the car. The thuds speeded up, going round and round the car, beating onto the back, side windows, even the front windscreen, and then round again.

The couple's immediate reaction was that there was someone outside. The car windows were slightly steamed up but they could still see through them. There was no-one outside.

And then the banging become so rapid that no human could have been involved. It would have been impossible for anyone to get around the car that fast, especially across the bonnet. Whoever it was would have had to splay themselves across the bonnet.

Michael's girlfriend started screaming, putting her hands over her ears to shut out the awful noise. The car shook with each thud on the glass.

Michael straightened up his seat, trying to turn the key in the ignition, in the age old instinct to flee.

He pressed the accelerator too hard and flooded the engine. It wouldn't start. He tried again, trying to swallow down his panic, trying to ignore the noise, the screaming, the rocking of the car, absolutely terrified himself. The engine started, and the noises stopped, as suddenly as they had started.

After the banging, the silence seemed just as unnatural.

Without exchanging a word, he drove away as fast as he could, his girlfriend still heaving with sobs.

It was all over in less than two minutes.

Years have now gone by, but Michael never did find out what had happened. There were no marks on his brand new car, and he and his girlfriend are certain that there was no on else around.

It was some time before they could even talk about it. But someone later told them that suicide victims had been buried in the ground by the chapel.

The chapel stands as it did, the only witness to what happened that evening, whatever it was…

Digging Up The Past

Sarah was like many other teenagers during the war. She still wanted to go out, to see films, to meet her friends. But the harsh realities of war had a way of taking over. Her parent's house in Sliema was destroyed by a bomb and they were forced to rent a house in Pieta.

It should not have been such a hardship. The house was, after all, huge. At the back of the building, a huge garden stretched out beneath the towering mass of St Luke's Hospital. And yet, something was not quite right.

When Carmen, her mother, first climbed up to the door and walked into the house, she would have sworn that something was barring her way. Nothing tangible, just a 'thickness', a pressure, as though an air-filled bag was inflated in the doorway.

The house had plenty of space for Carmen and her husband, Sarah and her younger sister, Joanna, and her other married daughter with her baby. She set about decorating it. The house was soon filled with huge, dark paintings, and old, imposing furniture that they managed to find here and there. Carmen may have liked the style, but Sarah found it oppressive, spooky.

And it was not just because of the furniture. The house was often shrouded in smoke screens let off to protect the boats in the nearby Torpedo depot, giving the place an eerie atmosphere even in broad daylight.

And on the wall on the roof they could see where some stones had crumbled and fallen. It seemed that lightning had once hit that spot, killing a man in the process.

And were the neighbours' stories true? Had someone committed suicide in the house?

Unlike Sarah, Carmen could not allow herself the luxury of allowing her imagination to run riot. They were lucky to have a roof over their heads. She was a pretty no-nonsense woman.

For some time, the family lived there and the

only change in their lives was the asthmatic wheezing caused by the smoke.

Until some people moved in next door. The house had an even larger garden than Carmen's and the family decided to start up a small weaving industry. Sarah and her sisters spent many hours sitting on their balcony that summer, draped over the railing, watching the men work in the garden next door. Sarah was quite a stunner and was quite aware of the admiring glances she was getting from the men below. But the harmless flirting came to an abrupt end when the men started cutting down a huge blackcurrant tree at the bottom of the garden.

The men had started to dig out the roots when their spades uncovered a gruesome sight. They carefully dug out the crumbling bones of a skeleton. Or at least most of a skeleton. Sarah and her sisters could hardly believe their eyes. Their hands flew up to stifle their screams. They watched in amazement as the men lifted out one long limb after another.

The men gathered around the bones and seemed to be discussing the find. They then casually tossed them into the pile of rubble which had accumulated against the adjoining wall and carried on digging.

"Ma, Ma!" the girls yelled as they ran indoors. "They've dug up some skeletons..." But Carmen would not have any of it. "Don't be ridiculous. It was probably a dog or something."

Sarah was about to insist but thought better of it. After all, she argued with herself, why on earth would a skeleton be buried under a tree... unless....

Her mind was filled with images of murders and strange disappearances. It was only later that evening that Sarah realised that the men had only dug up the limbs and torso. No skull.

Sarah's younger sister was studying for her school exams at that time and she used to help the neighbours' sons with their homework. It wasn't too difficult; they were only about 10-years-old and quite hard-working. So Joanna had no idea what their mother would want to talk to her about when, one day, she pulled her over to one side. "Have the kids said anything to you about a man?" Joanna stared at her blankly. "What do you mean?" she asked. It seemed that the boys kept complaining that there was a man wandering around at the bottom of their garden. The neighbour wanted to know whether Sarah and Joanna had ever seen anyone from the balcony.

Joanna mentioned it to her mother, but soon forgot all about it. Shame, really, as it was a warning of the things to come.

One summer evening, the girls were all sitting around the dining-room table, a sultry breeze blowing in from the open door to the garden. Carmen was bustling around the kitchen. She was a creature of habit and had little rituals that she followed regularly. Every evening, she would send the girls up to bed and follow a little while later with a tray of hot drinks and biscuits. But tonight, it was not to be.

She suddenly went deathly-pale and stifled a scream. "Sarah, shut the *antiporta*," she yelled and then, to the girls' bewilderment, she turned and ran out of the room, up the stairs. They heard the door of her bedroom slam shut and the key turn in the lock. And then there was silence.

They had no idea what was wrong. They tried to work out what could have happened but the only thing that Sarah remembered was the sound of the light-switch flicking on and off. Not that that would have meant anything. It was one of the days when they did not have any electricity and the room was lit by a large oil-lamp. And she also heard the door-handle rattle slightly after her mother left the room, but it did not open and she thought it was just the way her mother had slammed it.

The girls waited for a while and then realised that their mother was not coming down again. They were surprised. What could have frightened her so much that she would run away and leave her children down there?

It was not till the next morning that they found out. Even then, she was reluctant: "You'll go mad if I tell you." Eventually Carmen, looking fearfully around as she spoke, told them that she had looked up to see a smart, elegant man walk into the room from the garden. He was tall, dressed in evening wear.

And instead of a face, a skull grinned lewdly at her.

The effect on Carmen was profound. Whenever the girls went out, she would refuse to stay in the house alone, and would wait by the *antiporta*. She refused to talk about it again, but often Sarah would catch a look of horror flitting across her face. The ghost was obviously still in the house.

What is more, it seemed to have attached itself to Sarah. For weeks, Sarah would suddenly feel a coolness behind her. The light-switch would click on and off as she walked into a room and the door-handle would rattle. They once heard the sound of heavy, rasping breathing coming from their bedroom. But she never saw anything, and the door never opened.

Her sister one day flew down the stairs. Till

then, she had been pretty sceptical, but her face showed that something had changed her mind. "OK," she gasped. "I believe you. There is something there." She too refused to talk about what she had seen or heard.

The days passed, and their mother grew more and more fretful. In the end, the strain of the unwelcome visitor proved too much for her, and she had a heart attack and died.

The girls were beside themselves with grief. But the house loomed larger and more terrifying after that. They tried all sleeping together in one room, but in the end, fear got the better of them They decided to move in with Sarah's brother in Mellieha for a few months. Eventually, they gave up the house and moved into a far smaller place that the authorities managed to find for them.

The family did not really want any reminders of the house, but they had spent a small fortune doing it up. Sarah's married sister, Mariella, insisted on removing at least the bathroom fittings and some other bits and pieces. She was to regret her decision.

They all went into the house together, hoping to find safety in numbers. Mariella's little girl clutched her aunt Sarah's hand, aware of the strange tension in the air. As they all walked down the stairs, the little girl was suddenly snatched from Sarah's side and slammed against the wall opposite. No, she didn't fall. She was actually *thrown* horizontally across the stairs, banging her head, and falling unconscious to the ground. Even now, Sarah can remember with a shudder of horror the silence after she had fallen down onto the ground. Not even a cry. Mariella had scooped the little girl up into her arms and run out into the street with her, with Sarah and Joanna not far behind.

They never went into the house again.

The authorities immediately found three other families desperate for a roof over their heads. But even these families did not last long in the house. Sarah heard that one woman died soon after moving in. Her aunt told her that another woman had seen someone, something, while she was in her bath, and had run out into the street, terrified out of her wits, completely naked. The neighbours abandoned their weaving industry and apparently left the island.

And the house still stands. Sarah is now in her 70s and whenever she passes the house, she wonders whether the family who now lives there have ever seen the man with no face.

And whether the workmen who dug up the skeleton from under the blackcurrant tree could have had any idea of the forces that they had unleashed....

Minding The Baby

Anna and her husband doted on their new baby. Just before it was born, they moved from a flat into a large house in Valletta with splendid views over the harbour. They thought it would make a lovely family home.

The baby disrupted their lives, as babies always seem to, but they did not care at all. They soon settled into a routine and in the confusion of nappies and late-night feeds, they paid little attention to the strange things that started to happen.

A broom fell over onto the edge of the basin, knocking open the tap underneath, and water poured through the house. The first time it happened, they put it down to bad luck, perhaps a most unlikely thing to happen, but still just bad luck. But it happened again and again, once when Anna was out. She returned to find the whole ground floor flooded. The smell of gas would fill the house for no reason. The room upstairs would never warm up.

But the first incident that really shook them out of their apathy happened late one night. They had already gone to bed, bolting the huge front door that was so common in Valletta. They were amazed when it suddenly flew open. Leo ran downstairs and shut it again, but they had to admit that something strange was going on.

The next incident was even more worrying. Anna went out to church early one Sunday morning, leaving the three-and-a-half-month old baby asleep on the bed next to her husband.

"Make sure he doesn't roll over!" she fussed as she went out. Not wanting to point out that the baby could barely even raise his head yet, Leo just nodded.

"I'll keep my arm over him all the time," he reassured her.

He had only been laying down a short while when his arm flopped down on to the bed and the reassuring warmth of the gently breathing baby was replaced by the soft sheets. He sat bolt upright, trying to work out whether he had fallen asleep. Where was the baby?

Suppressing a moment of panic, he looked around and saw the little baby lying face down in the far corner of the bedroom, still fast asleep.

Leo looked at the baby in total amazement. He was sure that he had not fallen asleep and could still remember the suddenness with which the baby seemed to have been pulled out from under his arm.

And yet even if the baby had somehow managed to roll away, how did it fall off the bed and not even cry? And how did it get to the other side of the room? Leo had no explanation.

Little did he know how many other things would also perplex him over the coming years.

Once, at night, Anna heard a strange noise coming from the kitchen. Leo said: "Oh, leave it, it's probably just the cat."

But Anna went down to find that the loaf of bread had seemingly exploded, showering slices of bread onto the floor. But the slices were not spread everywhere as would have been the case if it had really just been knocked to the floor (what by, she preferred not to think). The slices were in a neat row, a narrow path of bread leading to the door.

Whatever "it" was, its sense of humour was tinged with a cruel, malicious edge. One night, when the baby was not yet a year old, Anna left him fast asleep in his cot. She went downstairs to get a bottle of milk ready for his next feed, but when she went up again, the cot was empty. She pulled away all the blankets in the futile hope that the baby could be hiding under them. He was nowhere in the room. Anna stood there, unable to think clearly, trying to figure out what could have happened, when she saw the baby's little hand waving outside the glass pane of the window.

The house had little round metal balconies, mostly decorative as they were only a foot deep. The balcony was linked to the room by a waist-high door, which they kept bolted, and then over it was a high window, closed with an old-fashioned latch attached to the vertical rod which rotated to lock the window at the top. The little stool that Anna kept near the cot had been pushed over to the window, and the heavy latch had been opened.

Outside, sitting in the balcony in his red pyjamas, his legs dangling between the metal bars, was the baby, the baby who could not even walk yet. Anna went white with fright. The balcony was five floors up; she preferred not to think about what could have happened as she pulled the baby inside and back into the safety of the cot. She preferred not to think about it, but how could she not, whenever she was alone?

Many people would have left the house there and then, but Leo was still sceptical. He was convinced that there was a simple, logical explanation for everything that had happened until then, but he had a hard time explaining how the baby had got out of his cot, pushed the stool, opened the window and got out onto the balcony,

They started to toy with the idea of leaving, but whatever was behind the incidents seemed to sense that it may have gone too far, and things quietened down for a while. Eventually, the years passed by, with only the odd incident. The broom kept knocking the tap open, and other little accidents occurred which might have been normal or not, but they were minor enough to ignore.

But then one night Leo was at work, and Anna had been reading in bed with her son asleep next to her. He was by now almost three-years-old, but still their only child and he often stayed in her room for one more story to be read to him when daddy was working late. Anna was on the phone with her cousin, when the sound of bells starting ringing through the house. The noise was loud, eerie, continuous.

Anna remembers her mother saying that they used to ring the bells like that when someone was dying. Eventually the noise became so frightening and deafening that she hung up on her stunned cousin and called her husband, begging him to come home, by then almost in a panic.

The dog, which normally hated bells and would bark madly, stayed fast asleep. She looked up. Across the door, a man passed by. At least, she thought it was a man. The figure was wearing a priest's *suttana*, but was only visible from the waist down. She has, even now 25 years later, absolutely no doubt in her mind that she saw him.

By the time her husband came home, she was absolutely hysterical, sitting up in bed, clutching her son to her, too terrified to even get out of bed and put the room lights on.

Eventually, it was her mother-in-law who forced them to make a decision.

"Ever since you have lived in this house, there has been something wrong," she insisted. "One of you is always ill, the doctor seems to be here every time I come round."

She brought an Italian exorcist down to Malta. He walked into the house, his brows knotted. He went all over it, trying to drive out the spirit with prayers, but as he left the house, he pulled Anna towards him and warned her in a furious whisper: "Leave this house as soon as possible."

That was all the prompting Anna needed. They virtually abandoned the house, leaving most of the furniture behind and moved into rented accommodation. As they left, one of their neighbours took the opportunity to tell them: "You know, no-one has ever been able to stay in that house longer than five years."

Anna looked at her in amazement. Why had she waited all those years before saying anything?

Eventually they found a buyer - not surprising really, as they had dropped the price to a ridiculous level. Leo warned the man about their experience, his conscience unable to stand the thought that something dreadful might happen, but the man sceptically shrugged his shoulders, more worried about whether the low price hid some dreadful secret about the drainage than the paranormal.

The time came when Anna had to face going in to the house to fetch her belongings. She clutched Leo's arm, and braced herself. For almost a year, she had refused to even walk down the street, let alone near the house. As she walked in, waves of emotion rippled through her. She had loved that house, she had had such wonderful plans for it.

"Why were you so cruel to me?" she thought to herself. As soon as she did, she was suddenly flung headlong, banging her forehead badly in the floor. There was no step, nothing that could have caused her to stumble.

And there Anna's story ends. They moved into a modern house and felt better than they had for years.

She later found out that the day the man moved into the house, his two children both fell ill. Within a year, his wife had died, his brother had been tragically killed, and he himself died a short time after.

The house has remained empty ever since.

Time Slipping Away

To this day Paul has no idea what it is about 1.45 a.m.

He just knows that there is something that wakes him up, not quite a noise, not quite a movement.

But one night remains set in his memory. He had come home at around 11 p.m. to an empty house. His parents were away on holiday and the 20-year-old was tempted to stay out with his friends, but he just wanted to get a good night's sleep.

The summer night air was stifling. He went straight to bed, opening the window wide to let in what little breeze there might be.

Paul lay on his stomach as he always did, covered only with a sheet, and within seconds he was fast asleep.

And then, he was suddenly wide awake. The room was still and silent. He had no idea what had disturbed him. He felt no traces of grogginess to indicate that he had been asleep. And yet, when he turned his head, the alarm clock on the bedside table said 1.45 a.m. He shut his eyes and tried to sleep but he was wide awake. Something was not right but it took him a few seconds to realise what it was.

There was silence.

Not the normal hush you would expect at that time in the morning, but rather a thick vacuum, as though all the normal sounds of garden, traffic and wind had been sucked out of the room.

Paul twisted his head around just far enough to look at the window beyond the end of his bed. The window was still wide open, but there was not a breath of air ruffling the curtains. Nothingness.

And yet outside it seemed to be almost dawn. Perhaps the alarm clock had stopped. He turned his head to look at the alarm clock, but it had disappeared.

What was going on? He stared at the bedside table. It had not fallen onto the floor. It had just vanished.

Paul lay still on his stomach, struggling to figure out what was happening.

And then he felt the sheet being pulled off him. It slipped down a few inches and then stopped. Had it been a blanket, he would have perhaps been able to blame the movement on its own weight dragging it down. But this was just a sheet and the sensation was certainly not of something slipping. If he had any doubt it was dispelled within the next few seconds. In spite of the balmy summer air, a cold shiver ran down his spine.

He is not ashamed to say that he was terrified. From the moment that the sheet started moving, he did not dare turn round, terrified of what he might see. His skin tingled with the sensation that there was something behind him. And the sheet was tugged down a bit further. He was frozen in terror, not even daring to breath.

What was happening?

And then with a sudden sigh of relief, he realised that it was probably just his cat. Of course, that was it. The cat would often sneak into his room and snuggle up on to the bed…

The door was shut, but perhaps she had somehow managed to climb in through the open window. He almost groaned with the relief of finding a logical solution. He got out of bed and padded across to the door to let her out, but as he opened the door, the cat slunk in, rubbing up against his legs as she walked.

He looked at her, unable to accept that his logical solution had suddenly been deflated. The cat leapt onto the bed and was about to snuggle down on the rumpled bedclothes, when she stopped suddenly and looked at the sheet, which was now in a pile at the end of the bed. Her ears pricked up and she bared her fangs. Without warning, she jumped off the bed again and disappeared through the door.

Paul was transfixed by the sight of the sheet. He looked at it as though he expected it to move. He has no idea how long he stood there. Eventually he took a deep breath and strode over to it, trying not to let his imagination drag him along on its flights of fancy. He took one corner of the sheet and tugged it off the bed, throwing it high into the air.

And there was nothing there.

Paul felt absolutely foolish. The fear started to ebb away and he checked the whole room, in the cupboards, under the bed. Nothing.

He got back onto the bed and decided it was warm enough to leave the sheet on the floor. No harm in being careful. He lay down, suddenly exhausted as the adrenaline rush of the past minutes drained away.

And then he noticed his alarm clock. It was on the bedside table again. He stared at it uncomprehendingly. The time was 5.15 a.m. Three and a half hours had passed since he had felt the sheet pulled off him.

Paul has never mentioned the story to his family and they still live in the house in Mdina. But he still often wakes up at 1.45 a.m. for no apparent reason.

Room Service

Whether you are a frequent tourist or an armchair traveller, few of us have not at one time or another envied tour-leaders, who get to visit so many dream destinations. To our mind, they only have to put up with the petty complaints of the group. But for one Maltese tour-leader, a trip to one of Europe's most picturesque spots, a place he had often visited before, was nothing short of a nightmare.

It was a warm, summer night in July. On Saturday night, he went to bed at around quarter to midnight, in a hotel he had visited often before. He left the small bathroom light on, just the one over the shaving mirror: a trick he had picked up over the years. Being a tour leader meant he had to stay in many different hotels, and the light helped him to find the bathroom in a strange room.

At about 1:30 in the morning he woke up and found that all the lights were on in the room: the ceiling light, the bedside table lamps, the main bathroom light, even the corridor light by the door to the room.

He didn't really think anything of it at the time. "How silly of me. I must have left everything on," he thought to himself. He just turned everything off and went back to sleep.

To this day, he has no idea how much time passed, perhaps just a couple of minutes. All he knew was that when he woke up the second time, the bedside lamps were on. Everything else was off. This time, he could distinctly remember having turned them off. A cold shiver of fear ran down his spine. But he shook it off - he was a grown man who often stayed at hotels on his own after all, and anyway, he was not convinced that he wasn't dreaming. In a moment of inspiration, he decided to write down on a piece of paper: "I switched off all the lights in the room."

But by then he was well and truly spooked and decided to try the opposite: turning on all the lights once again. He pulled the sheets up over his face and closed his eyes. The reassurance worked, and he dropped off again. But the July warmth made it too uncomfortable and he pulled back the bedding. All the lights were off. Every single one. The room was in total darkness.

He suddenly realised what people meant by the expression 'to have your blood run cold.'

Suddenly lying there in the dark, he could feel the breath of a large animal against his cheek, possibly a large dog. In the stillness, he swore he could actually hear it panting. He was completely terror stricken, his throat so tight he was unable to shout or scream. He tried to make a sound but couldn't.

All of a sudden the lights came back on. The room was empty.

As soon as his breathing got back to normal, he called the receptionist. It seemed to take an eternity for the telephone to be answered, but when the young man from downstairs answered he didn't know what to say to him, feeling foolish once the lights were on again.

"Yes, sir, what is wrong?" he asked.

"Something is wrong with the lights - they keep going on and off and there are things happening that I am not really happy about," the ashen-faced tour-leader said. "I'm coming downstairs."

He put the receiver back on its cradle, put some shorts on, and stopped only long enough to wash his face in the bathroom, still able to feel the warm breath of the animal there. He had no shirt on, and didn't even give a thought to his luggage. But as he came out of the bathroom, there was a sudden furious banging on the door of the room. He thought the door would come off its hinges.

He had to get out of the room, and the door was the only way out. After taking a deep breath, he found the strength and courage from somewhere to fling it open. There was nothing there. The corridor was silent, its deep carpet giving no clues. He staggered out, flicking his head this and that way to make sure there was nothing creeping up on him.

Even the idea of getting in the lift, where he would be trapped, was too terrifying.

He crawled down all four flights of stairs in shock. He has no idea how long it took.

All he knows is that by the time he got downstairs the receptionist was openly laughing at the sight of a grown man on hands and knees, seemingly terrified of the dark.

"What's wrong?" he said.

He told him about the banging, his voice sounding strange and hollow. The young man shook his head and smiled again. " Oh, that was probably an old man or something knocking on all the doors."

Standing in the well-lit reception, his story seemed plausible. "Come on," the receptionist offered. " I'll take you back upstairs."

He refused.

"Forget it. There is no way you will get me back in that room. You can keep the money I paid, but I want to check out straight away. I don't want to set foot in this hotel ever again."

To this day, the tour-leader is convinced that the terror of that night was not a dream. When they went up to get his bags, they found the note he had written to himself: "I switched off all the lights."

Eleven months later, he had to go to that village again. The hotel was all locked and shuttered. Was his experience just a practical joke? Or was it the reason that the picturesque hotel closed down? He will never know…

The Imaginary Friend

Annette's parents were troubled by the fact that she one day refused to sleep in her bedroom. She was only five years old and yet any attempt to get her to share her room with her sister resulted in tantrums and hysterics.

Thinking it was just a phase, they allowed Annette to sleep on a make-shift bed in their room in the house in Valley Junction in Msida. But it wasn't just a phase. Years went by and she still avoided the bedroom. Even when she wanted to get through the room to go to the bathroom on the far side of it, she shut her eyes and ran through as fast as she could.

But the situation got worse.

By the time she had reached the age of six, Annette completely stopped playing with her brother and two sisters, and started instead to spend all her time playing in the yard with her young friend. Together they would while away the hours, flicking marbles across the yard, dressing and undressing their dolls, whispering and laughing together just like any two friends of that age.

There was only one difference - Annette's friend was not real.

Annette now describes the little girl as being around six years' old, with fair hair, shoulder length and parted in the middle, tucked neatly behind her ears. But the strangest thing about her imaginary friend was that she was wearing a Holy Communion dress, complete with veil, every single time she saw her.

Annette admits that she thought it was strange, and often thought of asking her about it, especially as the years went by. This little girl was always sprawled on the floor in the yard, in her ivory coloured dress... But she never accepted the fact that her friend could not be seen by anyone else.

And there was something else about her that Annette found unnerving.

During the day, the two of them were the best of friends, but as evening fell, Annette would get afraid - the little girl would go upstairs to the bedroom or up the narrow spiral staircase to the roof. But Annette always refused to follow, having been warned countless time by her parents that the roof was not safe, as it was only surrounded by a low wall, parts of which were missing.

Until Annette was 13 years old, she just accepted her friend's presence, ignoring her family and other friends, locked in her imaginary friendship. She had turned from a cheerful, outgoing child to a withdrawn teenager, lacking the ability to communicate with others.

Her parents fretted continually about the effect of this on Annette. They tried everything to distract her, seeking advice from the trusted parish priest and teachers alike, but they could find no way to wean her off the relationship. Eventually, they decided to move to a larger house, away from the regular flooding that affected the area whenever it rained... and away from Annette's obsessive friendship.

When the time came to move on, it seemed that their gamble had paid off, that the little girl had been left behind, playing forlornly in the yard of the house, underneath the window of Annette's former bedroom. Annette did not refer to her again, slept alone in her own room, and eventually started to make other friends.

Her parents breathed a sigh of relief. They were so happy to have their daughter back to normal that they preferred to forget about those unhappy years, than to try to figure out what it was all about. Let sleeping dogs lie, they thought.

Years later, Annette went to the old neighbourhood with her mother and ran into a woman who still lived nearby. The elderly woman was curious to know why they had moved away - she seemed quite surprised when Annette's mother said it was because the house had grown too small for the growing family.

"So it wasn't because of the… the other things?" she probed gently if none too subtly.

"Well, perhaps it was," her mum admitted. The old woman nodded knowingly. It turns out that even the family who moved in after Annette's left some years later - just as their daughter turned five or six and started getting ready for her first Holy Communion.

The woman took Annette's hand.

"My sister lived in that house about 50 years ago. On the day that her daughter was supposed to receive her First Holy Communion, she had gone upstairs, all dressed up, and…. Well, she fell to her death, from the roof."

Just recently, Annette went back to Msida to look at the old house. She hasn't seen the little girl since she moved out of the house, but her memory still haunts her, stirred up by the tragic story.

The house is now abandoned, and is being used as a stable. Perhaps it is just because it was always prone to flooding and too uncomfortable to live in. Perhaps not...

The Bag In The Attic

It was November, back in the 1970s. When Sarah and Angela opened the door of the little cottage, they could hardly contain their excitement. The two 19-year-old girls were in Wales, studying at the medical school, based in the hospital just a stone's throw away.

The lovely 18th century cottage was a God send. Most of the other students were based at the other end of the rambling hospital, an incredible mile of corridors away. But this was at the "right" end of the building.

One of the two former hunting lodges on the building's estate, the cottage was small, just two bedrooms and a combined sitting/dining room. But it had all two teenagers would need and they quickly settled in.

Posters of Donny Osmond and David Cassidy soon livened up the sparsely furnished bedrooms and the few bits and pieces that they had brought with them gave the place a cosy feeling.

But the term was already underway, and the girls were plunged into the rigorous routine of lectures and ward rounds.

Time flew and it was April before Angela and Sarah decided to give the place a good clean.

The curtains came down and the dust flew. The girls set to their task with an energy that their respective mothers would have approved of.

But looking back, perhaps their thoroughness was not such a good idea after all.

Sarah climbed the loft ladder and pushed open the door into the attic. It was pitch black in there and it took a while for her eyes to adjust.

She spotted a light switch. The light from the dusty, naked bulb did not reveal any surprises. The whole place was empty except for cobwebs and a single, lonely-looking, brown suitcase.

Sarah walked to the suitcase and looked at it with some surprise. It was clean, not a speck of dust on it, and yet it must have been there for six months at the very least. She picked it up. Empty.

She took the suitcase downstairs, and showed it to Angela. Strange, they came to the conclusion that it must have been left there by the previous student and put the suitcase away in a cupboard. Before long they forgot all about it.

But then strange things started to happen. One night, Sarah was up quite late studying. Angela had long since gone to her bedroom and the sound of muffled music from behind her door had gone silent. Sarah decided to call it a day and padded on tiptoes across the cottage to the bathroom. She walked down the little corridor that served as their entrance hall, through the kitchen, past Angela's room and into the bathroom.

As she dried her hands there was a knock at the door.

"Oh heck," she thought. "I must have woken Angela up."

She opened the door but there was no-one there, just the empty, darkened sitting-room.

At almost the same moment, Angela's door opened and her sleepy face peered out.

"What do you want?" said Angela.

"What do you mean?" Sarah replied, confused.

"You knocked on my door." Angela sounded slightly peeved at having been woken up.

"I thought you knocked on the bathroom door," Sarah replied.

The two girls stared at each other across the dark room.

Neither of them could put the sinking feeling into words. It seemed better to pretend that nothing had happened. They both went back to their rooms.

It was not long after the "knock" incident that Angela was sitting in her room studying late one evening. She yawned and decided that she had done enough. Calling out "goodnight" to Sarah, she shut her door.

One of the disadvantages of an old house is the way everything gradually bends and sags out of shape.

To close her door, she had to virtually shove it with her shoulder as it would stick on a raised bit of the floor. She was fast asleep moments later.

She has no idea what disturbed her. She only remembers that she was suddenly awake and saw the handle on her door turn slowly. And then the door, as if cured of its old age and sagging hinges, glided silently open. There was nobody there.

Angela screamed. She refused to sleep in there again and moved in with Sarah for the rest of the night.

It was soon Sarah's turn, however. One night, she was woken up, feeling suddenly very cold. As soon as she sat up on her bed, two posters on opposite sides of the room fell to the ground with a crack. One she would have paid no attention to, merely sticking it back up. But two? At the very same moment?

Sarah spent the rest of that night in Angela's room.

The girls could finally ignore it no longer. Something was going on, but what?

One night Sarah walked out of her room to the shower, checking that the front door was shut and latched, as was her habit. And yet, just a few minutes later, on her way back, the door was wide open.

Even though the girls were already quite spooked by the things that had happened before, they still preferred to blame anything that happened on practical causes. They decided that someone had managed to get a key to the front door.

The hospital engineer was grumpy when they asked him to change the locks. "I don't know what you girls get up to with them keys. You're the third lot that have come to me to get the locks changed," he grumbled to himself.

Sarah and Angela looked at each other as the significance of what he had said sank in. The third lot? Had anyone else gone through the unexplained phenomenon?

The list of bizarre events grew longer. One morning the girls were in the kitchen poring over a recipe book trying to decide what to cook for dinner that evening. Sarah scribbled down a quick shopping list and dashed off, grabbing her books. Angela was going to clear away the recipe book but decided to leave it there, ready and open on the right page for later.

And yet, when they got home that evening, the book was in the sitting-room upside down.

There were several other times when things

seemed to have been moved about. Most of the time, the girls blamed them on their normal level of untidiness. But sometimes they wondered…

Not everything could be explained away rationally.

Take the electricity in the sitting room. Several times, the girls would be watching television, only to find themselves plunged into sudden darkness. The first time it happened, Sarah thought there had been a power cut and went into the corridor to get some candles. But the lights in the rest of the house were still on.

And so it would go. The lights would flicker and the picture on the television would disappear. Or the lights and the television would go off, just for a few minutes.

This time, the engineer was unimpressed.

"Can't be," he said. "Just one room? Never."

By now, the girls had come to the end of their study phase and were due to leave for their practical workphase. While they were away, the fierce winter of 1979 took its toll on the house, bursting the water pipes in the subsequent thaw. By the time they got back to Wales, they were put into alternative accommodation and never went into the house again.

But the story does not quite end there. At the hospital, they ran into the girl who had lived there before them.

"Oh, do you know you left a suitcase in the attic?" Sarah asked her, suddenly remembering the strangely dust-free suitcase they had found.

"Suitcase? No, I don't think so. I would have noticed that I'd lost it," she said.

"And anyway, I'm ashamed to admit that in the three years that I lived there, I never even went up into the attic."

So, the suitcase had been up there for three and half years without any dust settling on it. And all the strange goings on had started after they brought the suitcase down. Was it somehow linked?

For all they know, it may still be there, in a cupboard in a hunting lodge on the grounds of a medical school cum hospital. And maybe, just maybe, the engineer still blames the medical students every time he has to change the locks.

Spanish Spectre

Houses like that were few and far between. Huge houses with three storeys, plenty of room for grandmother and spinster aunts. And only 17 pounds per annum rent. The family leapt at the chance and moved into the house in Paola when William was only 8-years-old.

He was a budding artist, and when the family had already gone to bed, he would linger downstairs at the dining room table, doodling and designing. The cat and dog would sit by his feet, content in each others company.

Until suddenly, one night, their hackles rose and the two cocked their ears and stared at the black shadows under the stairs. William peered across the hall, but could see nothing. The animals, though, could obviously sense something that he could not. Whatever it was frightened them so much that they flew down the hall and when they found the back door to the garden closed, began to throw themselves at the door, again and again, spitting and snarling in a frenzied effort to escape.

That first time it happened, William was terrified. He scampered up the stairs to his bedroom and hid under his bedding.

But when it happened again, the next night, and the next night, he got so used to it that he just ignored the animals' nightly panic.

William was - and still is - a creature of habit. Getting ready for bed, he meticulously took off his clothes and laid them neatly on the chair. One night, he could hear the tap in the bathroom next door start to drip. By the time he had taken off his socks and shoes, the drip had grown faster, more insistent. By the time he actually got into his bed, the tap was full on.

That first time he heard it, he had rushed into the bathroom, only to find that the basin was dry.

But when it happened again, and again, he stopped going to check, aware that someone - something? - was playing tricks. Whatever it was seemed peeved that he could not be lured out of bed. One night, he heard a grunt and hot breath on his face. He jumped up, but there was nothing there.

William did not say anything about the stairs or the tap to anyone. He was sure that his numerous brothers and sisters would just tease him.

But then, stranger and stranger things started to happen.

One summer night, the heat was unbearable. His brother no longer lived at home, having joined the services and gone abroad. So he dragged the mattress off the extra bed and onto the floor between the two beds. He lay there with the window wide open, trying to get back to sleep. He had almost dropped off when a cat suddenly hissed in his face, giving him the fright of his life. He propped himself up on one elbow and peered under the bed, but it was not his cat. He shooed it away but the cat would not budge.

Under his brother's bed, there was a big, zinc laundry tub. He crept around it and grabbed the cat's tail, and almost screamed with fright when the cat turned round to reveal a man's face.

The man looked Spanish, with a long, drooping moustache, and was wearing a hat with a bobbled fringe on it.

William looked at it in horrified amazement and then the cat-person disappeared.

William would have thought he was losing his mind, but the rest of the family also became involved.

One afternoon, he was sitting down with his sister on the sofa at the bottom of the stairs, poring over a book. At first, William only saw a pair of legs coming down the stairs and hardly paid any notice. But as the person got closer to the bottom of the stairs, he realised with a little shiver than it was the Spaniard.

With a mocking smile on his face, the man walked over to the two children, bent over and placed a kiss on the trembling sister's cheek. William tried to push him away but the man just turned around, walked back up two steps and vanished.

And as if that was not bad enough, the Spaniard was not the only manifestation. There was also a woman, dressed in a long, black dress with a lace scarf hanging off an upswept hairstyle. Once, when his sister walked into the house, she found the woman hovering behind her mother, arms opened menacingly. She leapt in between them as her mother walked up the stairs into her room and the woman disappeared.

Her mother never realised a thing.

The Spaniard and the woman in the lace mantilla started manifesting themselves regularly, terrifying William's brother and sister by appearing in the mirror.

His father once saw his mother walk into the house and go upstairs without greeting him, only to see her walk in again a few minutes later. It seems the first person he had seen was not who he thought...

The grandmother once also peered over the stairs as she swore she could hear someone reciting the Rosary. Another time, she complained that she caught William's sister and her boyfriend entwined on the sofa. But William's father knew that they were not at home at that time.

One brother came to visit William's mother, who was sick in bed in her darkened room.

"Sit down there," she said, pointing to the seat by the bed. He gave her a strange look.

"I can't sit there," he said. "There's already someone there," he said with an apologetic look at the woman dressed in black who was sitting there.

The mother could not see her.

Inevitably, things finally came to a head. One night, the sight of heavy canvas flapping in the stairwell woke everyone up. Anxious heads peered around the bedroom doors. One of the brothers went up onto the roof but could see nothing. When he came down, the family looked at each other warily.

Until then, none of them had talked to each other about the strange events. William realised, with a touch of relief, that he and his sister had not been the only target of the taunting. One by one, they all admitted that they had seen and heard incredible things over the past years

Once the story was out, several new episodes came to light. One of the brothers was married and lived nearby. Faced by the terrified group all trying to explain what they had been through, he was sceptical at first. But he finally admitted that he would often pass by the house and see all the lights on in the house, even in the middle of the night.

The family started to keep together as much as possible. One dinner time was disrupted by the sound of water trickling down the stairs. But no-one had been upstairs.

When they went to check, the stairs were as dry as a bone.

But what could the family do? The house had been a splendid home but life was rapidly becoming unbearable. William's father tried to find somewhere else to live, but the only other thing available was a tiny flat and it would cost double.

The landlord, meanwhile, tried to find someone else to rent the house. Couple after couple came to see the house, but they always stopped in the hall and stared at the darkness under the stairs. They would inevitably make excuses and leave.

Although the family was sure that it would not achieve much, William was entrusted with locking the door at night, which he did as securely as possible, jamming a huge wedge in the door to keep it shut.

They decided to move into the same bedroom, as none of them was willing to spend the night alone. Instead of reassuring each other, however, they managed to frighten each other even more by recounting the things that had happened over the years.

"Call Raymond," one sibling suggested. Raymond was a cousin, a big, tall lad… He would certainly not be frightened by a few noises... Or would he?

He was called over and the family settled down upstairs to wait for him in desperation, as though his presence would solve everything.

The opposite happened. The spirits seemed to object to the family's united front and the door downstairs started to shake violently.

One by one, all the doors of the house were shaken, all the way up to the roof. The silence after the fearful noise was even more terrifying and when the doorbell rang, the family's nerves were so taut that they almost cried out in fright.

William went down to let him in, and was not really surprised to find the door open, hanging on its hinges. From the look on Raymond's face, he must have heard something as he was very reluctant to go in and made lame excuses about having to go home to get something to eat first.

William grabbed him by the arm and drew him in. It was more than his life was worth to let him get away.

He dragged him into the kitchen and put on the kitchen stove to fry him an egg. While it was cooking in the spitting lard, William took a tray of drinks upstairs to the family's communal bedroom. He had hardly gone a few steps when he found Raymond panting behind him.

"I'm not very hungry actually," he insisted. William knew better than to ask what had suddenly destroyed his appetite.

"I'll just go and turn off the stove, then," he said.

Raymond took his arm and pushed him back up the stairs.

"No need," he said

"Everything went out, the stove, the lights,… all by themselves."

William smiled to himself. No wonder Raymond did not want to be left alone in the kitchen.

It did not seem that this 6-foot tall lad was going to be much help.

It was not only William who was unimpressed by Raymond's presence. When he woke up the next morning, the tie that he had carefully draped over the end of the bedstead was swimming in the chamber pot at the other end of the room…

The glass on his watch was also burnt, as though with a cigarette.

But that was in the morning. That night was just as terrifying. All the family were woken up by the sound of footsteps going down the stairs and into the bedroom, even though there was nothing there. William was sharing a bed with his brother and to this day he is not sure whether the punch he felt in his stomach was his brother's knee or, well, something else.

At last, eight years after the ordeal started, the day came to move out. Relatives turned up to help load the truck and vans and William was very busy. He certainly did not feel like chatting to the curious neighbours.

But one of them was very persistent.

"William, why are you moving out? Is it because you saw or heard something?"

William did not really want to talk about it and in any case they had promised the landlord that they would keep the story to themselves. But the neighbour pulled him into her house and showed him something which chilled him to the bone.

It was a framed photograph of a mother and her

son. They were all dressed up for Carnival and had apparently been killed and buried under the stairs in William's house.

And their costumes? The woman was dressed like a Spanish noblewoman complete with a lace mantilla. And the son was wearing a fake moustache and wore a hat with a fringe of bobbles…

The Omen

I received this story by mail. It is not first hand and I don't know the writer - but I thought it was fascinating enough to merit inclusion.

"My grandmother was the daughter of a successful businessman who owned many of the large houses in Pieta. At that time, people used to marry at a much younger age than they do nowadays, at 15 or 16 years, and though my grandma did not have a fair complexion, nevertheless, she was her father's "blue-eyed baby". Her mother, who tried to minimise the sacrifice of being separated from her only daughter, encouraged her (not to say forced her) to occupy one of their large houses, some of which were vacant.

The young couple decided on a large one, if not the largest available, which had a yard and a garden, and in no time they got married. They lived happily in the house and after some 12 or 15 months, their first baby was born.

It was a healthy boy with blue eyes and fair hair, which made them very happy. Grandma's conversation with whoever she met was always about the "baby with the blue eyes."

Even the old milkman, with his herd of some 20

goats following him, heard the daily morning bulletin about the baby and the weather day in, day out, as early as 6.30.a.m.

One day grandma experienced the biggest fright of her life. She spotted an extraordinarily large, black snake crawling in the centre of her yard. She was really scared and did not know what to do. Grandpa had just left on foot to go to work in the Grand Harbour area. There were no buses or cars in those days.

The milkman was the first caller. Needless to say, the daily greeting was totally different to the normal ones. Very excitedly, and at the top of her voice, she told the milkman what she had seen.

But the milkman, in a very low tone, said: "Madam, yesterday you told me that your healthy boy is about three months old. I don't have the courage to tell you what's going to happen within three days of the snake's appearance..." and he quietly walked away.

Exactly three days later, the young healthy baby was a stiff corpse. Unbelievable.

Grandma insisted on going to the funeral and that was the last time she walked down the large doorsteps of her house. After a time, she came to know that years previously, two other young mums had had the same experience in that house! Who knows if the black snake has ever made a re-appearance?

This episode took place around 1870. It was personally recounted to me by my grandma before she died in 1932."

African Mystery

Kenya is a land of mystery, a mosaic of tribal culture and traditions that have defied scientific explanation for centuries. Their medicine and magic, their fears and taboos have been handed down from generation to generation.

But not all of them are benign, as an Indian who lived in Kenya around 25 years ago found out to his dismay.

Raju found his true love in Mombasa. He and his bride settled down and spent two blissful years, but then, without any warning, things started to go wrong.

At first the incidents were small and they ignored them, finding rational excuses. Looking back, they are not quite sure why things like papers or keys should disappear and then turn up in the dustbin. At most it was inconvenient; car keys would turn up again on a windowsill a few days after they had had new ones cut.

But then things changed and the incidents became more destructive. They would wake up in the morning to find his wristwatch smashed where it lay on the bedside table. The toothpaste would be squeezed out of the tube into the basin, and toothbrushes were found with their heads twisted over.

Raju and his wife eventually had to sit up and take notice. These were no longer things they could blame on forgetfulness. Things got more serious. One time the takings from the shop were missing. They found the money torn up into tiny pieces, spread outside.

Raju's mother, who lived with them, was on medication. Her tablets disappeared and, remembering the money, Raju went to check outside. Sure enough, there were the tablets, strewn along the ground.

It was with mounting fear that they realised there was actually a pattern emerging, and within a few weeks, the frequency of the incidents had increased until something was happening every day.

Perhaps inevitably, they began to blame the incidents on a poltergeist, and reluctantly admitted that he seemed to have a mischievous sense of humour. They were to rue their words.

They would find sand in their food, even though the beach was nine miles away, and another time would be unable to eat it because it had too much salt in it.

It became unnerving to walk into the house, wondering what they would find. In the end, they moved into an uncle's house. There at least, they felt they would be safe.

But it was not to be. The poltergeist followed. Raju would open the fridge and find a neat bite taken out of the food.

But the next phase terrified Raju's young wife, Sita. She opened her wardrobe and found her clothes had been shredded; not just torn or holed, but shredded into long, thin ribbons.

She hoped that the poltergeist had just picked on her cupboard by chance, but with a sinking heart the family realised that she had become the spirit's target. One day, the women were sorting out a pile of ironing and found that several garments had been ripped. Only Sita's had been touched.

The relentless pace of the attacks was beginning to take its toll on them. They did not feel it was fair to inflict their problem onto their uncle if there was no respite to be had at his home. Sinking into a bleak helplessness, they moved back to their own home.

Trying to outwit the spirit became a desperate game. They locked Sita's clothes into a large trunk with some other clothes and locked it. When they opened it up again, only her clothes had been ripped. They realised with grim satisfaction that they had almost fooled the spirit. They had purposely put in some slippers belonging to Raju's mother that were very similar in style. The spirit had taken a few nips at them before realising that it was being tricked. Sita's were ripped to shreds.

The attention became even more focused and it was no longer only her belongings that were being threatened. She would wake up and realise with a shudder that her earring hoops had been squeezed out of shape. The spirit became more bold. She would feel a strange sensation as she was eating and look down to realise that her clothes had been frayed where she sat.

She became obsessed with the idea that she had brought the spirit into the home with her. It was hard to reason with her, to point out that they had been in the house for two years without any incident...

She and Raju flew to her family home in Zanzibar. It was so reassuring to talk to her parents who scoffed at the stories. Surely everything would be all right, so far away? But even her sceptical parents shuddered when they saw her clothes hanging on the washing-line, ripped to shreds.

It was no use. She was convinced that the spirit was jealous of her marriage and felt that it might have moved with them only because Raju had accompanied her. She would get no peace until he went away from her.

Raju was not terribly keen on the idea, but he

flew back to Mombasa and waited anxiously for the phone call which would reassure him that Sita had somehow broken the spell.

There had not been any attack that day. Could Sita be right?

Day followed uneventful day and still Sita was spared. The tension which weighed her down seeped slowly away with each tick of the clock.

But she could not hide, far from her husband. The word "curse" had sprung into everyone's mind; no-one could even say it out loud, so terrifying was the thought.

The family needed help. They called a spiritual society and eventually a Muslim priest, who listened to the Hindu family politely, realising how desperate they must have been to seek his help.

"You must realise that if you try to get rid of the spirit, it might work," he warned. "But it might also make it more angry."

Which would it be? They did not have too long to wait. Sita woke up to find bloody scratches down her arm. The next day, the next arm was gouged. The next day she watched in horror as scratches appeared across her belly. The next day, it was her legs.

She began to think that she was losing her mind, that she was somehow hurting herself in a fit of hysteria. They called a doctor in to treat the wounds, and Sita watched him carefully, sure that he too thought that she was hysterical. But the spirit was clearly warning the family not to confront it. As Sita pulled up her sleeve to show him her arm, blood oozed in little red drops from a scratch that spread down her arm, as though someone was pulling the sharp point of a knife along her skin. He fled.

There was nothing the rest of the family could do. Sita sank into a deep depression, driven almost insane by her unseen, unknown attacker.

The months passed, and well-meaning friends were put in touch with a variety of people believed to have special powers. Raju carefully copied out holy writings on the wall, but these would have disappeared by mornings, leaving only a faint scorch mark on the wall.

One man brought a mysterious looking tin with him, which he assured them contained a secret concoction which would drive away evil. He left it on a windowsill but it disappeared from there soon after he did. He was deeply upset to find the tin waiting for him on his desk when he returned to his office. He refused to return.

A sense of frenzy was building up. The family knew that a showdown could not be too far off. A blind man was recommended but the day he visited watches and clocks disappeared from the house, only reappearing once he left.

The spirit – if that is what it was – started to warn the family off, and they could hear the ominous sound of a blade falling onto the floor in the still of the night.

They felt they had tried everything... except tribal medicine. Swallowing their reluctance and instinctive fear, they made an appointment with a witch doctor who lived some 70 miles away.

That morning, the family woke up feeling more optimistic than they had in years. Everything will be OK, they tried to reassure each other.

But their optimism was short-lived. On the shiny, polished glass-topped table in the centre of the hall a footprint appeared. It was over 13 inches long, and Raju could only describe it with a shudder as "not ordinary".

The sweaty imprint lingered for a full half-hour. The family put the last few things into the car, hardly aware of what they were doing. They piled into the car and raced off down the long, straight road, hardly paying any attention to speed limits, weaving in and out of the traffic.

And then the brakes failed. The family found themselves sitting in the car, strangely silent, with clouds of dust still swarming around the car after Raju's heroic effort to control the skid. No-one was hurt, at least not physically. But the expression in Sita's eyes told of a much deeper hurt. Could they beat this... this Thing?

And yet they were determined to get to the witch-doctor. They felt that the footprint and the severed brake-line were a sign that they were getting close to a solution, that the Thing was feeling threatened.

They knew all about witch doctors and their strange incantations but still watched in fascination as the old man burnt feathers, deeply breathing in the fumes until he fell into a trance, mumbling incoherently.

When he opened his blood-shot eyes again, he stared intently at Sita.

"I know the spirit that is tormenting you and he will not leave you alone until he is happy. I will give you a necklace to wear with chants on the beads."

It did not seem to be much of a weapon against the evil that they were fighting, but Sita was ready to try anything.

She almost gave up when the attacks continued, a small cut in her tongue, a slight nick on her chest.

She had suffered for so long that she could hardly believe it when a whole day passed without incident. But then another passed and another and the family breathed a deep sigh of relief.

Six months passed and the family was lulled into a glimmer of hope that the ordeal was finally over.

Sita began to function again, getting out of bed, taking over some of the cooking duties. Raju caught his wife humming in the garden and felt an overwhelming sense of relief that his life was returning to normal.

Alas, it was not to be.

The attacks on Sita started again. In desperation they wrote to the witch-doctor asking for his advice. His son wrote back to explain that his father was very ill but that he would come to see them.

The man did not have the same awe-inspiring presence as his father, but the family waited patiently.

"There is nothing I can do. If my father could not help you to get rid of the spirit, then no-one else can," he ended with a shrug of defeat. "You just have to rely on your faith. You must believe that you can make it disappear."

The ordeal had lasted four years. After the witch-doctor's son left, Raju and his family put all their energy into willing the spirit out. They had beaten it for six months; they felt they could beat it forever.

The attacks grew milder and less frequent. Eventually they stopped.

It was a long, long time before they could pick up the strands of their life. It was years before they dared to talk about their story, terrified that mentioning it might somehow open a crack through which the evil could return.

They moved away from Kenya soon after and can scarcely believe the horror of those relentless days.

But sometimes as Sita is getting changed, Raju stares at the scars still visible on her arms and belly. They catch each other's eyes and shudder.

CHAPTER FOUR

Another misconception is that ghosts are the spirits of dead people. This story is about someone who was still alive, who had a message to pass on.

One Last Look

English Harbour in Antigua is a typically lush Caribbean Harbour, a tourist paradise, with fringes of golden beaches strung like pearls along the edge of the island, mangrove trees dipping their branches into the clear, blue sea.

It was a beautiful setting for a holiday - but one that did not just attract the expected type of guests.

I was working as a crew-member - and living on board - a 90-foot sailing yacht, not one of those sleek, fibreglass ones, but what could kindly be described as an "old tub".

"Valdivia" at the time offered air-conditioned luxury, miles of highly varnished wood that was stripped back to bare wood and re-done every season, even a telex machine at a time when they were still a novelty in offices, let alone a boat. But the boat had far more humble origins. It was originally part of the Baltic fishing fleet, way back in the Second World War and it had been bought by a young German officer. He had had the boat converted to sail-power, and we, like the many crews who worked on the boat before us, wondered why he had spent so much time and effort on the "tub"

In April of that year, we were particularly busy, trying to get the boat ready for the Atlantic crossing, making good the damage of a busy charter season in the Caribbean. That kind of work demands equally heavy relaxation, so when we all stumbled down to our cabins one night, pretty exhausted and a bit worse for drink, no-one expected to stir before the next morning.

But the cook, Marietta, woke up just after midnight and trudged down the corridor, past all the closed cabin doors, to the toilet, stopping to let a man pass her. It took a few moments to shake off sleep and realise that he shouldn't really be there. At first, she thought he was just a friend of someone on the boat - but it didn't seem likely. He was elderly, very tall, over six foot, white-hair cropped so short as to be almost military. Not quite Caribbean boat-bum type. Her doubts materialised as fear even as he dematerialised. He just went right through a corridor wall.

Needless to say, the "alarm" was raised - but no-one could take Marietta's story seriously. Who would, after a good night on the rum punch?

Nothing more was said. She gave up trying to persuade the sceptical lot of us, and apart from lying in wait for each other shining torches under our chins and surprising each other with woeful moans and groans, the incident was forgotten.

But weeks later, another girl, Irene, walked up into the saloon to find a man sitting there at the U-shaped table, which had a huge mirror on the wall behind it. She too hesitated, but as she started to walk towards him, she realised that there was something wrong with the scene in front of her. The man had no reflection in the mirror.

It all happened so quickly. She turned away in surprise rather than horror and when she turned towards him again, he was gone.

Yet again, cynicism won the day and the incident was put down to a fervent imagination, perhaps sparked by overheard stories from Marietta... So no one was surprised that Irene's man resembled Marietta's.

But what happened three weeks later was much harder to explain. By then eight of us were half way across the Atlantic, some 1,500 miles from land and, as every evening before the night watch took over, we were all gathered around the huge saloon table having dinner together. We had been very lucky with the weather - the seas were rising and falling gently and there was enough wind to keep the sails full, but we had not picked up another ship on the radar since a few days after we had left the Caribbean, and outside there was just an inky darkness. We used to look forward to washing up in the scant basinful of water each of us was allowed every night, slipping out of our dirty T-shirts into clean ones, and getting to chat to each other. During the day, some of us were on watch, some of us slept, others worked on the wood, sails, or engine. With so many of us living in such cramped quarters for so long, we each respected each other's need for privacy and a bit of space. But by evening, we were looking forward to a bit of company.

Valdivia had a raised saloon, with huge square windows along two walls looking out over the sidedecks, a far cry from the round portholes associated with sailing boats. I had my back to one of the windows, chatting to the captain, Steve, opposite me. He was in his mid-forties, a pragmatist who had made his fortune as a specialist diver and who now owned and ran Valdivia as his business. In the middle of a sentence, he just looked over my shoulder and shuddered in shock. Again, the whole scene moved tremendously quickly. We all spun round, aware that he had seen something outside the window, but expecting it to be the light of a ship. No one believed him when he said he had clearly seen the face of a man peering in through the glass. Not even when he described him as being an elderly man with white hair.

A search was immediately mounted for what must have been - what we hoped against hope had been - a stowaway. But even as we opened sail-lockers and checked whether any food was missing, all eight of us realised with sinking hearts that it was no real person that Steve had seen.

Eventually, after trying to re-create shadows and reflections with all manner of light combinations in a last desperate attempt to find a rational explanation, we gave up, and the incident was duly entered into the log.

Very little was said. After all, if we worked ourselves up about the fact that we were on a haunted boat half way across the Atlantic, there was not much we could do about it. We wouldn't exactly be able to move out, would we...?

So the night watches doubled up for the rest of the trip, and the summer went on without any further sightings of our uninvited passenger.

Till then, even we did not want to believe the story. But at the end of the season, the boat stopped off in Porto Ercole on its way to Sardinia and we met our charter agent who had also handled the sale of the boat from the German to Steve. Had we heard, he asked, that the German had had a stroke and had died? Steve replied that he had had never actually met him in person, the sale of the boat having been handled through agents and lawyers.

Apparently, the agent added, he had been in a coma for several weeks, from around the middle of April until the end of May.

By this time, the rest of us had perked up our ears and quietened down. A shiver ran down my spine. We all moved closer so that we could hear the rest of the story.

One of us hesitatingly asked what the German had looked like. And yes, he had white hair, cropped very short; quite tall, over six foot tall. He loved the boat, said the agent. Don't you think he would have loved to see the boat just one more time before he died...?

CHAPTER FIVE

Maltese folkflore abounds with stories of the hares, *a ghost who was often dressed as a Turk. The story goes that the* hares *would leave money for the woman to find, and that if she told anyone, the money would turn to either cockroaches or snails, and he would beat her.*

I found the legends hard to believe. Everyone knew of some old relative who had had a hares *in the house, but why were there no modern tales? Was it possible that the story of the* hares *was invented to cover up for the extra money a woman earned on the side, money she might not have wanted her husband to know about? Was it possible that a* hares *became a face-saving way to explain a battered wife appearing with a black eye?*

It may be just a coincidence that the hares *as a myth faded away as women were given more rights, as it became more and more unacceptable for men to treat their wives as chattel.*

There are only a few stories of hares *and Turks. See what you think...*

Turkish Fright

The most common form of ghost in Maltese folklore seems to be a Turk with a missing finger, who offers money to one of the family members, usually the mother. Known as the *hares*, he would threaten the person with physical violence if they ever told anyone about his presence. The source of money would also dry up. There are many stories of people finding tin boxes full of money under a loose tile somewhere, just as the *hares* promised, only to open them one day and find only empty snail shells or cockroaches. The *hares* was incredibly vindictive, according to the stories I have heard. One person told me about a whole room full of wedding presents that had been inexplicably smashed, in a locked room with no open windows through which a cat might have crept in. There were many, many stories of women who appeared with black eyes, refusing to say who was responsible.

But most of these stories are second-hand, recounted by great-grandchildren who remember *busnanna* rambling on and on. This is the first time I came across a first-hand account of a Turk appearing, and even then the context was different.

It was just a normal night, like any other. Daniella's father had closed the dog up in the bathroom and she and her parents were fast asleep in their flat, high above Tower Road in Sliema. Originally the area was the site of one of the oldest buildings in Sliema, but now the flats were modern and offered all the latest conveniences.

But perhaps something still lingered from the site's past...

In the dead of night, the dog suddenly woke them all up with his furious barking. One after the other, the bedroom doors opened. Daniella's mother was tying the belt of her dressing gown tightly around her waist, and her father stood trying to shake off his drowsiness in case there was something wrong. But there did not seem to be anything untoward. All the doors leading onto the wide corridor that they used as a 'common room' were still shut, and there was no noise from outside the flat that could have disturbed the sleeping dog.

Daniella's father walked over to the bathroom to let the dog out and see what was wrong.

But if that was the situation as the parents saw it, it was certainly different for Daniella and her dog.

All this time, Daniella had stood transfixed at her doorway, her mother standing silently beside her. But when her father walked across the corridor, she had to summon up every last bit of courage to stifle her scream.

Couldn't he see him? He had walked right through him...

For Daniella could see, in the middle of the corridor, the hazy figure of a Turk.

He seemed to be a grown-up and was wearing a turban and a deep purple, richly embroidered shirt. He was full size although his legs were virtually transparent and Daniella does not remember whether they were firmly planted on the ground or not.

He stood there with his arms folded, looking straight at her with an expression of curious amusement, as if waiting to see what she would do.

Daniella was frozen in terror. She was praying inside, hoping against hope that she was imagining things. She turned her head away but when she looked back, the grinning Turk was still there. She tried closing her eyes and opening them again. Still there.

Daniella realised from the way that her parents were staring at her that they could not see the stranger in their midst. They must have thought she was crazy. But she couldn't have been. The dog knew that there was something there too. It was still barking madly, chasing around and around the corridor, sniffing at the bottom of all the doors.

The few minutes that had ticked by since the dog had woken them up seemed an eternity to her. But then she decided to stare at the Turk, hoping to somehow intimidate him. It must have worked. With a final grin, he evaporated into thin air.

It was a while before she could speak. She grabbed her mother's arm: "Didn't you see him?"

"Who? What did you see?" her mother asked, taking hold of her terrified daughter's arm.

It was only then that she realised that the dog had calmed down.

No-one had seen the Turk, and had it not been for the dog's inexplicable reaction, Daniella would probably have persuaded herself that she had been seeing things. But the memory of the Turk's impudent grin stayed with her for a long time afterwards. She would suddenly feel a strong sense of oppression, of fear, and it was only by closing her eyes tightly and praying inwardly: "Please, please, don't come back again!" that the feeling would ebb out of her, leaving her feeling tired and drained.

Did she really will the Turk to stay away? She will never be sure. The incident happened when Daniella was in her late 20s. Over 10 years have passed. The family still lives in the flat and none of them has ever seen or heard anything unusual again.

Double Take

Vanna was busy at the kitchen sink when she spied her daughter going up the stairs to her room.

"Emma, could you get me down your dirty washing, please?" she shouted up to her.

Emma ignored her.

"*Iva*, Emma, answer me please. Will you bring it down?"

Again, no answer. All she heard was a little chuckle.

Moments later, her daughter came home. She insisted she had not been inside the house at all in the last hour or so.

Vanna shook her head in frustration. It was the *hares* again.

This playful spirit was always playing tricks on her, pretending to be one of her 11 children and sometimes making her wonder if she was losing her mind.

Another time, she saw her son Wenzu combing his hair in front of the hall mirror.

"Wenz, if you're going out could you get me some eggs, please?"

The youth just peered into the mirror, straightened his jacket collar and went out without acknowledging her.

Not sure whether he had heard her or not, she dried her hands on her apron and ran outside behind him. In the road, two of her children were playing with some friends, but there was no sign of Wenzu.

"Where's that brother of yours?" she asked.

The children looked up in surprise.

"He hasn't come back, ma. I haven't seen him since this morning."

The number of times she saw someone who turned out to be far away at the time, the number of things moved around of their own accord… all the incidents started to get on Vanna's nerves. She was getting obsessed with the whole thing. She never told her children anything about the *hares* but she confided to her husband that she had had enough.

Reluctantly, he accepted to move. They rented out the house and her husband organised a team of relatives to help move the big, heavy furniture to their new house, just a few doors down the road.

Vanna sincerely hoped that the *hares* would not follow her there.

As moving day approached, Vanna was exhausted. The spirit seemed more mischievous than ever and she heard his little chuckle of delight several times whenever he had managed to trick her.

By late afternoon, she sank down into one of the few remaining pieces of furniture, a comfortable, comforting old armchair.

Her head sank down onto her hands and her eyes shut, heavy with the straining of the day. As she sat there relaxing, she felt someone slip her heavy earrings out of her lobes, and she breathed a sigh of relief, until she realised there had not been anyone there. She opened her eyes. Her earrings were gone.

She called in two of her children and started looking all over the armchair. They lifted the cushions, checked down the creases of the chair, on the floor.

They lifted the chair to check underneath it, but they were nowhere to be seen. The children, who knew nothing about the *hares,* just thought that their mother was getting tired, until they too heard the little chuckle.

As Vanna sank back into the armchair with tears of frustration in her eyes, she and the children spied the earrings, at virtually the same time.

They were dangling from the ceiling above her, with nothing to hold them there, just defying gravity.

The ensuing frenzy of activity was farcical. The children were dispatched to fetch a broom and the three of them jumped up and down, trying to knock the earrings off. But "off" what?

Once they hit them, they fell to the ground and Vanna hurriedly slipped them back into her ears. It was the final straw, or so she thought.

She called out to the children and rushed out of the room. But her husband knew nothing of all this. He called to her to light a few paraffin lamps as it was getting too dark for them to see what they were doing.

Vanna would have preferred to leave the house, but she sent the children on ahead and lit the first. As she went to the second, the first blew out. She re-lit it and yet again, as she moved to the second, the first was blown out.

By now furious and frustrated, she lit it for the third time, and this time, in front of her husband and a few of his relatives, the lamp was suddenly smashed by a piece of wood which appeared from nowhere. Glass shattered and paraffin sprayed all over the floor.

Silence fell across the room. No one moved for a few seconds. Vanna stood there as white as a sheet, shaking from head to toe, still holding the lighted taper... Eventually, one of the men moved, frightened of the naked flame and the leaking paraffin.

The taper was blown out and Vanna was led away to her mother's house down the road until the remaining furniture was removed.

She never went back into the house again.

The *hares* did not follow Vanna and she never heard any stories from the people who moved in. Perhaps he has moved on. Or perhaps he is still sulking.

Possessive Urge

Rita had a lovely spacious house, on the main road of a village in the south. Most of her children had been born there and she felt it was her home. For a while, at least. But Rita could not stand it any more. There were just too many strange things going on. After six years, she decided she had had enough and moved out. She would probably have persevered and tried to put up with her *hares'* tricks - until he started messing around with her children.

One of the first things she remembers involved a little picture of the Sacred Heart of Jesus, which she kept on a window-ledge on the stairs. In front of it, she kept a wick alight, floating in a little glass container of oil and water. Once as she walked past it, the container flew off the sill and crashed in front of her, splashing oil and water everywhere. She thought she must have knocked it unconsciously with her arm - until it happened again and again.

She started getting quite jittery.

Rita used to keep all her towels in a huge chest of drawers, all neatly folded and sorted out. Once she opened the heavy drawer and her cat leapt out with a squeal, giving her the fright of her life. She was sure that there was no way the cat could have got in there without her noticing.

On another day, when her younger daughter Carmelina was only three-years-old, she left her asleep in her bed and dashed across the road to the little shop. She only had a few things to buy; it couldn't have taken her more than 10 minutes at most. Which was certainly not long enough for anyone to get all the carpets out of storage and laid.

And yet, that is exactly what happened. She rushed in to check on Carmelina, but the little girl was still asleep, alone in the house.

"Oh well," she said to herself, bemused.

"I suppose I should be grateful that I have been spared all the hard work…"

The *hares* was very defensive about the house. The original house had been twice the original size, but it had been split into two. The landlord once wanted to reallocate some of Rita's room to the house next door. The *hares* seemed to have different ideas. When the landlord came over to measure up, the wooden door would not budge, even though it was not locked and the room was in constant use. As soon as the exasperated landlord left, Rita went upstairs again and the door opened effortlessly.

She never actually saw anything, although her son constantly complained to her about interruptions while he was trying to get his homework done.

"Ma, ask him to shut up!"

Nor did the hares ever give her anything, even though he cost her a fortune in broken crockery.

And then her daughters got involved.

Her 10-year-old daughter was in the cellar, doing her homework on the table there. All of a sud-

den, the three shelves under the window all collapsed, crockery and ornaments crashing to the
ground. She would have blamed it on faulty nails,
but her husband checked them all carefully and
could find no reason to explain their sudden col-
lapse.

The *hares* took a liking to the children. The house
had a flight of stairs leading up to the washroom on
the roof. Whenever the two girls came down from
there, they would feel themselves lifted up into the
air, and they would float down the flight of stairs, a
few inches off the ground.

This did not just happen once, but almost every
time they went up there.

"I didn't like it," Carmelina told me. "But neither did I mind. We were kids, we just accepted it."

As she told her story, she stood up, hunching up
her shoulders to explain what she meant. She said
with a smile: "When we moved into the next house,
for a long time I still hunched up my shoulders
whenever I was going down stairs, ready to fly. But
of course, it never happened again."

Her sister's experience was perhaps a little more
frightening. Not only did the *hares* "fly" her down
the stairs, he also suspended her upside down.
Carmelina remembered her pinned up against the
wall, head down, about two or three feet off the
ground, her feet in line with a small, flower-shaped
window that overlooked the stairwell.

Carmelina was not going to be spared completely though. In winter, they used to close off the
entrance to the cellar stairs with a large wooden
board, to keep out the cold, damp air. She was once
walking across the board when it just evaporated.
She fell into the cellar, but when she got up and dust-

146

ed herself off, luckily unhurt, the board was still in place.

The *hares* was sometimes merely teasing, playful. Her elder daughter once called out to Rita from her bedroom upstairs. But as soon as she answered, her daughter appeared behind her, wedged into the corner of the room.

Three brothers, who used to live a few doors away, refused to play with Rita's children any more. One of the teenaged boys was convinced that Rita's son was hitting him whenever he walked by. But Rita knew that there had never been anyone in the house at the time... At least, not anyone from her family...

Eventually, Rita had had enough. She brought a maid in to clean the house and moved out, leaving much of the furniture behind. She shut the door behind her with a sigh of relief.

But it was still not all over: the *hares* had another trick up his sleeve. The next time Rita met the landlord, he expressed his surprise that she had left the house such a mess. Apparently, he had found cat excrement in every room..

Carmelina lowered her voice and leaned forward.

"The woman who moved in after us.. Well she kept rabbits in the cellar and once when she went down there to get one out, she found it had been turned into a dog."

Her memory of falling through the wooden board obviously still clear in her mind, she added: "Once she fell into the cellar and broke her back and both her legs."

When this woman moved out, it seems a tailor took over the house to use as a workshop and even though he was only using the hall, he too moved out soon after.

The house is still empty.

The Dwarf

"I'll go!" David said, without hesitation. The eight-year-old was the only one of 12 children who really enjoyed staying at his grandmother's house in Mdina.

She was now in her 80s, and living alone, and David's father worried about leaving her on her own at night. Most of his children were too young to be of any use to her should she need anything, but David was one of the eldest.

None of the children had any specific reason for not wanting to go there but David really enjoyed it,

He slept in a little gallery overlooking the large sitting room, and he could pretend he was anything he wanted to: a sea-captain, a soldier, a fireman.

Below him, the room was large and quiet. Huge paintings in thick, heavy frames virtually lined the walls and he looked at them with the hushed awe of childhood.

He was quite happy playing on his own in the silent time until he fell asleep. And he certainly did not expect to be awakened.

But one night something did disturb him and he opened his eyes. There was someone in the room. He could hear him moving around.

He sat up in his little bed and peered over into the room.

A little dwarf was leaping around the room, jumping from the top of one portrait to the other, working his way around the room. He was only about two feet tall, and seemed weightless,

He was wearing green trousers and a white shirt, with a sash around his waist. He had no hat on, so David could see his pointed ears quite clearly And his shoes had long, curling tips to them.

David rubbed his eyes, sure that he was still asleep, but the dwarf ignored him. Eventually, David grew bored watching him and fell asleep, in the way that only a child could.

The next day, he was sure that he had dreamed the whole thing and he did not mention it to his grandmother.

But the next week, when he went back there to spend the night, he was once again woken up by the little dwarf, skipping merrily from portrait to portrait.

This time, the dwarf noticed David. It stopped, and with a cheeky grin, hopped down onto the ground.

It wandered over to one of the large floor slabs, and beckoned David down.

David did not move at first.

The dwarf kept jumping up and down excitedly, and eventually David's curiosity got the better of him and he wandered down.

The dwarf pointed at the slab once again.

The slab looked like any other, but when David got down on his hands and knees, he realised that it was loose. He lifted it up, and found, underneath, a lovely, shiny coin.

He had never seen such a valuable coin and grabbed it, replacing the slab carefully, but when he got up again, the dwarf was gone.

He waited for a while, but the dwarf did not reappear and he went back to bed, falling asleep soon after with the coin clutched in his fist.

The next day, he remembered his dream as soon as he woke up.

Except that it couldn't have been a dream, because in the palm of his hand was the large, shiny coin.

David gave the coin to his grandmother. She had never seen anything untoward in the room, and there were no other secrets stashed under the floor slab.

Old wives' tales do say that if you tell anyone about secret gifts of money that you will never find any more.

To this day, David, now in his 40s, wonders whether anyone else ever saw the little man with the pointed ears again.

Another family still lives in the house, in one of the rambling alleys behind the cathedral. Perhaps they have never said anything, worried that their source of money might dry up.

Perhaps not.

Threatening Turk

Aunts can be very fond of their nieces. When the aunt in question is childless, then they can be very fond indeed, pouring out on their relative all their maternal instinct. Such was the case with Rosa. She adored Consiglia, and made sure that the little girl came over to see her as often as possible.

By the time Consiglia was eight, she would spend several afternoons a week there, following her aunt around.

That particular afternoon, there was a pleasant breeze blowing, and Rosa tried to get as much of her laundry done as possible. Consiglia traipsed up the stairs behind her to the roof, but Rosa never really felt comfortable with the little girl up there near the *cint*, and so she made her sit in the wash-room at the top of the stairs while she hung up her load.

Consiglia didn't really mind, but there wasn't much to do. She eventually found a piece of plaster and started drawing little pictures and patterns on the floor. She started singing quietly to herself, total-ly un-self-conscious in the way that eight-year-olds have.

And then she spotted him. A handsome, 20-year-old boy, standing at the bottom of the staircase. He was dressed as a Turk, not the turbaned, baggy trousers type, but as a soldier, with a red skull-cap, edged in black with a black tassel, and an immacu-late uniform. He had in his arms a huge cardboard box, and he took the lid off with a flourish to reveal what seemed to the little girl to be paradise itself: layer upon layer of brightly-wrapped chocolates.

The Turk smiled benignly and proffered the box to the girl at the top of the stairs. Consiglia was tempted, but the message about taking sweets from strangers had been well drummed into her head. She looked through the door behind here at the roof but could not see her aunt.

"No, thanks, " she said.

The Turk leant his head over to one side, lifting one eyebrow enquiringly, and held out the glittering sweets again. This time, though, he took a step up, as though approaching her. Consiglia couldn't explain why – his friendly expression had not changed one jot – but she suddenly felt quite frightened. And yet the chocolates rustled enticingly in their cellophane.

"Put it down there, and I'll come and take them," she decided.

The Turk just looked at her.

"I'm afraid. My aunt will be angry with me," she added.

And then the Turk took two or three steps up, and said calmly: "Take!"

Consiglia was overcome by a shudder. She put her hands over her ears and screamed. She screamed and screamed, eyes screwed up in fear.

"The Turk is going to take me! The Turk is going to take me!"

Within seconds her aunt was behind her, a look of anxious concern on her face. She enfolded the shaking child in her arms and rocked her backwards and forwards until Consiglia stopped sobbing.

"I don't understand these children. One moment she's happily talking to herself and playing, the next she's screaming," Rosa muttered to herself.

As soon as she stopped crying, Consiglia fled outside, leaving her aunt at the top of the stairs. She told her aunt what she had seen but nothing that her aunt said to re-assure her could convince her that the Turk was not hiding just around the corner of the stairwell, or that the box was not still lurking on the bottom step. Rosa shook her head, and went downstairs to have a look around, but even then, Consiglia refused to budge. Rosa began to get a little impatient. She scooped the little girl up into her arms and carried her down the stairs. Consiglia covered her eyes, burying her face in her aunt's comforting shoulder.

Consiglia never saw or heard the Turk again. But as time went by, she was to learn that there were many other strange occurrences in the house. Her uncle would often find his wood-working tools moved around in his shed, and there were often strange noises that the family could never really find a logical explanation for. Consiglia stopped going to visit her aunt, and to this day still feels uncomfortable near the house.

She found out that the family that lived in the house before her aunt used to hear the sound of a bird's wings flapping violently in one of the rooms, but never found anything there. And they often heard the sound of a girl crying.

Whatever there was in the house, her aunt could not take it and soon moved out to Cospicua. The house belonged to the family and another aunt lived there after the Turk episode. She was once woken up by a terrible nightmare. Or at least, that is what she tried to persuade herself that it was. There was a woman in her room who shrieked madly "I'll stay here until I kill you all. You'll all die here."

Nightmare or not, the prophesy seemed to come true. Her grandmother and grandfather both died in the house, and even her aunt Rosa was brought back to the house to be looked after during an illness and died there.

Several other people moved into the house; none ever stayed any length of time. There is now a foreigner living in the house, and Consiglia once ran into her and told her about the strange Turk. She did not seem at all phased by the idea, quite the contrary.

Seventy years have passed since Consiglia saw the Turk and she is still fascinated by the episode. "If I close my eyes, I can still see him as clearly as I did that day on the stairs. His smart buttons, the tassel on his hat. And that box of chocolates.

"I would love to have the chance to go back to the house, to see if I could feel anything. But I have always been too shy to ask... But I do wonder," she said, "what would have happened if I had taken one of those chocolates."

She shuddered. She evidently didn't think that it would have been anything good.

CHAPTER SIX

Many ghosts are the spirits of those whose lives have ended prematurely, always traumatically. Whether a murder, a suicide or a tragic accident, these ghosts seem unable to find rest.

Why? Perhaps when a person dies naturally, their energy dissipates slowly and gradually. What if this process does not occur when a death is sudden, quick? What if that energy persists as what we call a ghost?

Lingering Sadness

The house was big and rambling. It dominated a whole corner of the block in Valletta. The family had been very happy there but a feeling of uneasiness began to fill Mary. She was by her own admission a very superstitious type and eventually she could stand it no longer, she called in a *bahhara* from the south of Malta.

The ancient custom is, in a way, a mild form of exorcism. The Maltese strongly believe in the evil eye, and the *bahhara* is often called in to walk around the house, burning blessed olive leaves on a plate. It is believed that the pungent smoke drives away any evil spirits that may be lurking in the house.

On this occasion, the family solemnly followed her from room to room, mumbling prayers as they went. But then as she went into one room, the smouldering leaves suddenly burst into flame. The fire leap up a foot into the air, so suddenly that the *bahhara* almost dropped the plate. The rest of the family let out screams, quickly muffled as they watched her.

She walked all around the room, taking step by measured step and finally, she looked up.

"Someone has been murdered here," she proclaimed. The family shook their heads in disbelief. They had never heard anything untoward about the house. The *bahhara* was adamant. As if to give weight to her statement, as soon as she stepped out of the room, the flames died down suddenly to a smoulder once again.

The flames flared up slightly once again in another room, but this time, she smiled. The feeling was a positive one and not a negative one. She walked around the room and stopped in front of a photo of Mary's mother-in-law which sat on the fire-place mantelpiece. The flames played gently.

"This woman really loved you," she announced. "She is a very strong presence."

The mother turned to the rest of the family gathered at the doorway.

"Yes, yes," she agreed. "She was a very strong woman, determined, may she rest in peace. She cared a great deal for me, she was such a help."

The *bahhara* wandered around the rest of the house, and left without any further incident. The pungent smell lingered in the rooms.

But it was not just the smell which lingered. Mary was unable to get the memory of those flames leaping suddenly in the air out of her mind. A murder indeed! The very thought!

A few days later, Mary went to the corner shop and stopped for a chat with one of her older neighbours on the doorstep. Lowering her voice confidentially, she told her that the *bahhara* had been round. Her neighbour nodded approval.

But when she mentioned the strange sudden fire, her neighbour looked quite pensive.

"*Mela*," she said eventually, her deep wrinkles creasing even more than normal. "Well, I remember that where there is now a garage, there used to be a little shop. And yes, there had been somebody murdered there. I remember all the police. Oh, yes, there certainly was a murder there."

The flames had risen in the room next door to the garage.

The sceptical will dismiss this story. Had the *bahhara* just done her homework and spoken to someone before going to the house? It would have been so easy to add something unnoticed to the leaves to make them burn suddenly.

There are many in Malta who would, however, believe that the *bahhara* had just done what she is meant to do: seek out the spirits in the house.

Desperate Secrets

Antoinette was just about ready for a cup of tea. Much as she loved shopping, it was tiring work. Even for a teenager.

When she stopped outside her friend's house, just off the main shopping road, and they sorted out which package was whose, she leapt at the offer of a drink. Still chatting together, Helen put the key into the lock of her front door.

Antoinette's heart almost stopped. No sooner had she opened the door than a sound of wailing and ferocious shouting started up from inside. It was a hideous noise, loud and terrifying.

Antoinette turned to Helen but was surprised to notice that her face was registering embarrassment rather than shock.

"It is nothing," she said. "There is nothing there. Don't worry."

She opened the *antiporta*, and sure enough, the wailing stopped immediately.

Antoinette took a step back, still terrified, not daring to look into the dark hall. Helen walked into the house.

"Look, you see. There is no-one here."

She reluctantly took a hesitant step inside, waiting for her eyes to adjust to the dark after the bright sunlight outside. The hall was empty. The clock ticked reassuringly in the corner.

Her friend shrugged. "It happens a lot. I suppose I am used to it now."

She explained that the heart-rending shouts would start up as soon as the family stepped through the door but stopped as soon as they opened the *antiporta*. They had never seen or heard anything inside the house. Helen took Antoinette's hand in hers.

"Please," she begged her. "We never even talk about it amongst ourselves. Please, don't say anything about it to anyone."

Antoinette found it hard to put the awful wailing out of her mind. Perhaps that was why she had such a vivid dream that night.

She dreamt that she went into her friend's house and a man, dressed in black, appeared at the top of the stairs, beckoning her in. He seemed to be quite elegant, wearing a black cloak and a wide-brimmed hat. He had something in his hand; she thought it was a scroll, tied up with a red ribbon around it.

As she went into the house, the man spoke to her, instructing her to tell Helen to dig up the floor under the third floor tile from the *antiporta*. "If you do," the man continued, "you will find riches beyond your wildest dreams."

Antoinette woke up with a shudder. Although the man had promised her money, the atmosphere of the dream had been evil, threatening. The next day, she still felt really disturbed by the dream and wanted to tell Helen about it. She went to her house and started blurting out the story almost as soon as she had got inside. As soon as she saw her, Helen also started blurting out a story about a dream she had had. It was not long before the two of them trailed off into silence. They had had virtually the same dream.

In Helen's dream, the man also dressed in

black - had told her to dig up part of the floor, but he did not say anything about money, and he also told her to dig up an area under the stairs.

Helen had also been upset by the dream. She and Antoinette went to the foot of the stairs and looked at each other. What should they do?

Helen told her father about the dream. Perhaps there was something unusual, some intensity or hint of panic in her voice, as she recounted the improbable story, because he took the advice in the dream seriously. They decided to dig up the area under the stairs.

It is hard to know what the family were expecting to find. It was certainly not the legs of a skeleton. In shock, they carried on digging and underneath, found a pile of crumbling skeletons, laid in a shallow grave under the stairs.

The family found out that there had been some unexplained disappearances in the house. It seems they had found evidence of some long forgotten murders.

They did not know what to do about them. The idea of the publicity, the effect on the value of the house, the psychological trauma of finding out more details of whatever had gone on... They couldn't cope with it. Eventually, after much soul-searching, they decided to cover the skeletons up again and to keep the whole incident as quiet as possible.

Perhaps the evil had been laid to rest. Antoinette never found out any more. Helen refused to discuss the matter and never even said whether the voices were ever heard again. For all Antoinette knew, the skeletons were still there.

Many times over the years, Antoinette remembered her dream and toyed with the idea of asking

Helen to dig up the third tile from the *antiporta*, but she never dared.

But sometimes, when Antoinette walked her friend home and Helen put the key in the door, they caught each other's eye and shuddered.

Antoinette died over 13 years ago, but she often told this story to her family when she was still alive. Helen's family still lives in the house.

Unrequited Love

George and Joanna found their dream house just in time. They were just about to give up, having seen countless houses, none of which had that 'something special' to set it apart.

This house was superb, large and rambling, the oldest part probably over 150-years-old. It was in a bad state, having been uninhabited for seven months, but they could immediately envisage what it would look like. They set to work immediately, their enthusiasm growing as the house and garden took shape. Everything seemed fine, until it came to moving in their furniture.

The removals-men had carried in most of their belongings, and there was only about an hour's work left. But it was getting dark and the men refused to go into the house. One of them, looking decidedly sheepish, admitted to George: "We won't go in the house. It's haunted."

George was an utter sceptic. "Codswallop" was his only comment. But they would not relent and the work was continued the following day.

Yet he was intrigued by the story and started asking around the village. A story gradually emerged of an Elizabethan knight whose ghost had been seen wandering around the house. He had a good laugh to himself over the whole thing and forgot about it.

And at last, the house was ready to move in to. Their two children had bedrooms downstairs and they slept upstairs. About a month later, his mother came down from England to stay with them, and George's son was moved out of his room to make way for his gran.

She was a lovely old lady, "a real character" he liked to say. She arrived late one evening and it was really only the next day that George had a chance to catch up on all the news. At one point, she asked who else was staying in the house.

George did not realise why she was asking, and said that there was no-one else there, prattling on about wanting to settle in properly first and so on.

"Oh, I see," George's mother continued. "Then you had a visitor, did you? Eleven o'clock was rather late to be calling, I thought."

"Visitor? No, there wasn't anyone here," George insisted.

"Yes, there was. I had to go to the bathroom and came out of my room, and there he was in the corner of the hallway. I was rather embarrassed to find him there, I wasn't even wearing my dressing-gown," she explained. "I did stare at him at first. He was terribly good-looking. I think he must have been to a fancy-dress party as he was dressed in those funny shorts and tights. I nodded a greeting, and he nodded back," she continued, unaware of the effect her little bombshell was having on her listener. "But by the time I came back from the bathroom, he had gone. I came back out of my bedroom again a bit later to see if I could find him - he *was* ever so good-

162

looking. I looked up the stairs, but he had gone. I suppose he came down from your room and got confused about where the front-door was, turning left rather than right."

And then she realised that George was looking at her in bewilderment. There had been no-one at the house, no visitors. He could feel the hair at the back of his neck prickle.

"Oh dear," she said, after he had told her the story about the removals-men. "I wouldn't tell Joanna and the children. They'll refuse to stay here."

But George did not have to tell anyone. It soon became quite clear that the whole village knew about the ghost, and they always found it difficult to persuade locals to come to the house. For years, they could only persuade male babysitters to stay overnight, and even their daughter would not stay alone in the house.

Joanna tried to defuse the situation, calling the ghost "Percy" which she felt was appropriate for the era he seemed to belong to. With time, they eventually managed to talk about "Percy" to their friends; it became a great dinner-party story, a bit of a laugh.

Until about five years ago. By then they had lived in the house for over 20 years, and apart from the one episode involving George's mother, no-one had actually seen or heard anything again. And then there was a knock at the door.

A rather frail, elderly English lady stood there, and she politely introduced herself as Anne, saying that she had lived in the house as a little girl. She asked whether she could speak to the owner. George had been working in the garden and she had obviously assumed that he was just the gardener. There was a momentary embarrassment but it was quickly dispelled when she spotted the huge tree which now towers over the corner of the garden. "Oh, I remember when the tree was the same height as me," she said.

They worked out that she had lived there almost 70 years before. She was obviously curious to re-visit her childhood home and George and Joanna were quite happy to show her around and hear more about its history. As they sat down over a coffee, George thought this would be the perfect opportunity to ask about the ghost. He was perhaps a little disappointed when she said: "Ghost? Oh, no. What rubbish. There was never anything at all."

Anne left soon afterwards but a few weeks later they got a lovely card from her. In it she thanked them for their hospitality. And then she launched into a little story.

"I said that our years there were some of the happiest in my life. But perhaps that is not strictly true. In the last three months of our stay there, my father was very busy, working with the Services, and was away from home a lot. My mother met a handsome naval officer and fell madly and deeply in love with him. My sister and I were aged 12 and 14, old enough to be aware of what was going on. We were truly terrified that mother would leave us. But she did the right thing and did not run away with Tom, as he was called. In later years, she did admit to us that it was a great struggle.

"You may wonder why I am telling you this. Mother died in the early 1970s and it seems that Tom died around five years or more before her. And it is most curious. Apparently mother and father met Tom and his wife at a carnival ball at the Royal Opera House. And Tom had been wearing

Elizabethan dress. I wonder if he could be your ghost?"

And a story which could so easily have remained a dinner-party anecdote suddenly became a story of a passionate, unfulfilled love. For they had moved into the house in 1969, just around the time that Tom died. Had he come to look for his lost love, hoping for the time they could be together again? That is what George and Joanna would like to think. And they no longer joke about "Percy" any more.

CHAPTER SEVEN

Some spirits just want to be left in peace. These stories are about ghosts that come back to plead for the sanctity of their resting places.

A Simple Candle

When Erica first went to the house in Mdina, it was for a friend's housewarming. She was only in Malta on holiday, but the house felt immediately right to her. She could not get it out of her mind, she felt so welcome there...

A friend, sick of hearing about the house, had a brainwave and encouraged her to ask the owner whether he would be interested in letting her use it for a few weeks every year.

Erica was overjoyed when he said yes. In 1977, she finally stayed there alone for the first time.

She found it impossible to explain why she loved the house. It was only small by Maltese standards and the downstairs part, which dated back to the 13th century was dark and gloomy, full of shadowy corners.

But it was not this foreboding ground floor which was haunted. It was upstairs.

The first floor was older, having been added on after the earthquake in 1693.

Erica knew immediately which room was to be hers: a large room with oak beams, flooded with light from the central courtyard. It had a small annex at one end, which led to a narrow spiral staircase. She realised with a grimace that the staircase was too narrow to be of practical use (she couldn't manage to negotiate the steps with a laden tea-tray) but that bedroom it was to be.

She soon found that someone else still thought of it as their favourite room.

One night, she was woken up by the sound of sweeping. It was a rough, grating sound, as though whoever it was, was using a birch broom. At first, lying there in the dark, she thought the noise might be the wind, but it was a still, calm night. It was too regular and recognisable a sound to be written off as plumbing, and it was certainly not coming from outside.

Who on earth would be sweeping in the early hours of the morning? Totally unafraid, she turned on the light. There was nothing, no one there. And the sound of sweeping stopped straight away. She waited for a few seconds, wondering if she had dreamed it all, but as soon as she turned off the light again, the sweeping started rasping yet again.

Over the years, she was to hear the noise over and over again.

She never saw anyone in the room, but once, when a friend was staying with her, she went downstairs to clear away some of the cups and glasses from the bedroom and she is sure that she saw a dark figure walk through the kitchen. There was nothing beyond the room except the outside toilet.

She called up to her friend to make sure that it was not her she had seen: "I've just seen something rather funny," she said calmly.

She was quite worried that someone might have got into the house, but the kitchen was empty and so was the toilet. She shrugged it off without a second thought.

Over the years, other friends came to stay with her and many regularly heard the sweeping and rustling.

Most of them found it very disturbing. No-one could really understand why she felt so good about the house. Many of them shuddered and refused to go into the bedroom at all. The husband of one of her friends only made it as far as the bottom of her lane.

"Don't you find it a depressing house?" she was constantly asked.

And she would always reply: "No, I love it!"

Her curiosity was aroused. She tried to find out whether there were any rumours connected with the house. All she could find out was that the children next door used to say that an old lady had once been pushed down the stairs by a ghost. She did find out that a lady had in fact fallen down the stairs and had been certain that she had been pushed. But nothing remotely sinister every happened to Erica.

A friend of hers was psychic which seemed to encourage the ghost, which started whistling behind the visitor whenever she was standing in the kitchen. For the first time, footsteps were heard.

Erica and her friend were once at her neighbour's house for tea and her friend said with a shudder that she was quite afraid of the house.

"Nonsense," said the neighbour, "they wouldn't hurt a fly."

Both Erica and her friend stopped mid-sentence and looked at the neighbour.

"So," asked Erica. "You do know something…"

The neighbour looked sheepishly into her cup of tea.

"Well, perhaps the ghosts are trying to tell you something."

Apparently four people, a man and his three sisters used to live in the house (the neighbour thought it might once have been a bakery) and that one after the other had passed away a few decades before and were buried in a small nearby chapel. The neighbour hesitated, and then added: "I was in the church recently, arranging some flowers, when I noticed that their tomb had no candle on it."

The parish priest looked up in surprise when Erica walked into the chapel carrying flowers and a votive candle. But he did not attempt to talk to her. No sooner had she laid them down on the grave of Mary Anna, one of the sisters, than her friend said that the mood in the house seemed to lighten.

But the house had more mundane problems than its ghost. It was getting old and dilapidated and the time came when Erica had to think about moving out. The ceilings were leaking and one of the walls was collapsing into a nearby garden. Erica was quite emotional about the inevitable parting. She had got used to the idea of someone standing behind her and had got used to simply turning and asking: "What is wrong"

She would often go into the shadowy room at the back of the ground floor and sit in total, inky darkness, feeling calm and protected.

But she had to move, and the ghost responded to her emotion.

The pungent smell of incense wafted through the house as a sort of final gesture. She walked through the bedroom into the small room. The small slab in the corner was slightly more worn than the rest from countless night-time sweeps.

It was not Mary Anna, she was sure of that. She, at least, was at peace.

And suddenly, the image flashed through her mind of some dark secret, perhaps some mentally disabled child who had long ago been left chained in the corner.

Once the image had been conjured up by her imagination, she could not get it out of her head. She fetched a small candle and lay it slowly on the floor and suddenly it felt as though the oppressive feeling of that corner was sucked out of the house.

Was it all her imagination?

The house was still there the last time she came to Malta in the 1990s, albeit in an even worse state. She went to stand in front of it, unable to tear herself away from it completely.

Later that afternoon, she was sitting in a nearby tea-room, and overheard some people talking about the house.

"What became of the haunted house?" they chattered.

She smiled to herself. To her the ghost was far removed from the scary phantoms of people's imaginations.

It was part of that lovely house and she could understand why Mary Anna had left a part of herself behind her. Erica felt that she too had left a little part of herself sitting on the stairs, listening to the overflowing silence of the house.

The Desecrated Grave

Censina was a devout Roman Catholic. Every night before she went to sleep, she knelt by the bed in her house in Paola and recited a litany of prayers. But it had been a very busy day and her eyes seemed heavier than normal. Her prayers for the dead trailed off into nothing and she decided to give in to her fatigue.

She had not been asleep for very long when she awoke to find her room flooded with light. She looked at her clock, but no, it was the middle of the night.

And then she heard it. The sound of voices raised in prayer. A man's voice would start the prayer, and the chant would be taken up by the murmurs of a crowd. The sound seemed to be getting closer and closer.

She got out of bed, pulling a shawl around her shoulders as she shivered, partly from the cold night air, partly from fear. She crept to the window and looked out. The road was filled with a ghostly parade of souls, all carrying candles. The procession stretched all the way down the road to the Addolorata Cemetery and was moving, slowly, down her road.

Terrified by the chanting spirits, she ran back into her bed, pulling the covers her head: "Dear Lord! Give them eternal rest," she whispered breathlessly, over and over again.

And all of a sudden, it was dark and silent again. The souls had been granted another night of peace.

****

Crash. The sound of breaking crockery resounded round the small courtyard. Crash. The noise was alarming, and totally unexpected and Angela jumped up from her desk and ran to the door.

There was no-one around, both the cooks had gone home some time before, and yet the echo of the shattering noise still resounded eerily in her mind.

She ran downstairs from her first floor office, trying to listen through the door of the locked up kitchen but there was total silence.

"A cat," she thought to herself. "I bet a cat has managed to get in there."

It was 1981. The kitchen had only just been finished. It had been excavated out of the rubble at the bottom of the historic fort, rubble that had once formed part of the splendid bastions.

Angela waited for a few seconds but the noise had stopped. Shivering slightly, she went back upstairs to her office, built over the kitchen in a more modern part of the complex. "Modern" is relative, of course. The original fort dates back to the 18th century but other parts had been added on by the British.

As soon as she went back upstairs and sat down at her desk again, the noise rang out again, echoing through the silence. Crashing, splintering, smashing.

"That cat must be going mad," she fretted, thinking of the mess the next morning. Still, there was nothing she could do, no key and no-one she could contact.

The next morning, she went straight to see the head cook, Anthony. He was whistling when she went in, obviously unperturbed. There was absolutely nothing out of place. Not a single thing was broken.

Angela explained what had happened and Anthony looked suspiciously around the kitchen, but the other cook, Fredu, was not as sceptical.

"Don't tell me any more because I warn you, I won't stay here on my own," he muttered. "There is something very strange going on here. I keep hearing all sorts of noises…"

But what could it have been?

A little while later a visiting Englishman, who had been based at the barracks there during the war, told her that the fort was linked to a neighbouring hospital through a maze of underground tunnels. Legend has it that in the time of the Knights, a scullery boy had built up quite a reputation for being clumsy, dropping crockery and breaking plates far too often, as far as the kitchen and nursing staff were concerned.

Once, after he had been even clumsier than normal, the nun picked up her broom to whack him, but he darted around her skirts and ran into the tunnels to escape her wrath. He never came out again.

Surely it couldn't be him, his desperate spirit endlessly replaying the disaster which drove him to his terrifying, lost wanderings, trying to find his way out…

Still Angela was not one to let her imagination run away with her. She was often in her office working late, and apart from that first time, she never heard the breaking crockery again.

But the place did have an atmosphere…

Late one afternoon, not long after, she went into the little bathroom at the end of her office, in the oldest part of the building. As she stood at the basin drying her hands, she felt someone looking at her and spun around. There, just a few feet from her, a man was peering at her through the little window.

"His eyes were so dark, so piercing," she remembers.

"He was dressed in black, at least the part of him that I could see, which was just from the chest up. But he had longish hair, shoulder length, and a little pointed beard. His face was terribly sallow. Really pale," she said, without a trace of fear. As she looked at him, the face just faded away. She ran to the window but there was no-one around and no way anyone could have climbed up to the window in any case. Angela didn't tell anyone, preferring not to let other people achieve through their fears what her imagination had not.

Weeks passed and the office was getting ready for its Christmas festivities. A young woman came up to her office and asked whether her father could come and have a chat. Apparently he had been based at the fort for some time and wanted to reminisce. The man was now quite frail, but he lowered his voice conspiratorially.

"So, has anyone seen the Black Knight again?"

Angela jumped. He continued, pointing at the picture behind her of the fort being bombed during the war.

"You see that? The bomb hit the chapel and the commandant sent some workers in to fix the roof. But after a few days, they sent a representative down to complain that they would not do any more work until a man, who kept turning up on the site, stopped annoying them.

"The commandant was a man of the world, not one given to superstition, but he soon realised that the man in black they were complaining about was no real person. He said nothing to the workers, though, realising that they were blissfully ignorant of the visitor's nature…

"The commandant waited until they had left and then went out to the chapel. He climbed down into the beautiful carved crypt below the chapel only to find that the tombs had been desecrated. Vandals had pulled the covers off the graves, and bones were scattered all over the floor. He spent hours putting everything back as it should be, and he said that, after that, the man did not appear to the workers again."

Angela shuddered, thinking about the man's face at the bathroom window. She waited till the next morning and climbed down the steps to the crypt.

Her hunch was right. The graves had been disturbed.

Fortunately, there were no bones left to replace, as she doubted whether she would have had the courage to pick them up, but she organised a team of workers to straighten the slabs of intricately carved marble. Brushing the dust off their hands, they left the crypt. The man did not reappear, but she was sure that he was content, not gone.

She often heard footsteps on the wooden planks that ran behind one of the rooms. Once, after she had locked up the office, turning off all the lights, one of the staff looked at her strangely as she came down the stairs buttoning up her coat.

"Are you leaving that man alone up there?" he asked.

"What man? I've been on my own all afternoon," she replied.

"Just now, as you were coming down the stairs, a man was still walking around upstairs. I saw him through the window," he insisted.

They both warily went up the stairs, unlocking the door, and turning on the lights. Needless to say, the office was completely empty and quiet.

Angela says that neither the breaking crockery, nor the Black Knight ever frightened her in the 15 years since then.

Only once did the atmosphere catch up with her.

At around 3.30 p.m. one afternoon last year, she was filled with an inexplicable dread and fear. She knew that she just had to leave. The feeling was impossible to ignore and she turned everything off and went home early, not daring to glance back at the dark stillness.

The next morning, when she came in to work,

there were two rows of burnt out candles along each side of the road and a circle of ashes in the centre of the car park. The police were there in force, taking notes and measurements. It was presumed to be some kind of Satanic ritual.

How had she known? What mysteries had the midnight visitors hoped to uncover?

The crypt is now bricked up and the site is slowly but inexorably falling to pieces. Angela is sure that one day, strange noises will again disturb the silence of the fort, and that the Black Knight will have cause to rise again, wanting only to be left in peace.

Saving The Monument

Josephine was in her 80s when I met her, still sprightly and sharp. She had always been interested in learning as much she could about everything around her, and archaeology was just one of the subjects she had adopted.

She learnt in a way most of us would envy: through none other than experts Sir Temi Zammit and Lord Strickland. When she was younger, she would go with them on their 'digs'.

Perhaps because she was there when Malta's substantial heritage was literally being unearthed in the second decade of the 20th century, she gained a deep respect for the civilisations of the past which had so painstakingly created these monuments to their beliefs.

One of her favourites is Hagar Qim. She was at that time still involved in various groups who met there to pray. Perhaps it was this respect which made her the logical choice when someone from the past wanted to make contact…

Many years before, she had gone down to Hagar Qim with her son and his British wife. The couple wandered down to Mnajdra, but Josephine preferred to wait for them at the top, having visited the site quite often. The place was quiet, deserted, and she decided to sit down in the shade.

She was at first quite surprised when a man appeared by her, as she had not seen anyone else around, but she was even more taken aback when he addressed her by name.

Sitting next to her, the man said: "I've come to see you, to ask you a favour."

She looked at him. He was neatly dressed in a pale blue silk shirt, with dark trousers, and she noticed that he was wearing a skull cap. He had a neatly trimmed, pointed beard, and although he looked slightly foreign, he spoke impeccable English.

"I understand that you are a friend of the Prime Minister, Dom Mintoff," the man said.

"Yes," she said, again surprised at his knowledge of her.

He paused slightly.

"We need to talk to him, to ask him not to hold any more shows here at Hagar Qim."

A few events had been in fact been held there, with multi-coloured lights, dancers and pop songs. Hagar Qim was truly a marvellous, dramatic setting for it, but it had crossed her mind more than once before that it might be sacrilegious to hold such events at places of worship, no matter how ancient.

Who was this man, though, and why was it his concern? She felt it was only her right to ask.

"I am a Jew, a rabbi," he said.

"Very well," she said, after only the slightest hesitation. "I will call Mr Mintoff tomorrow to pass on your request, but first you must tell me where you have come from and how you know my name."

"I come from the Ancient Jews," he explained. "We are distressed to see all these things going on here. For us, this is a very holy place. We are the sons of Abraham. When we were taken to Egypt, half of us escaped and took to the sea. We took with us whatever scrolls we had, our families, slaves and tools. We needed to find a place to build our temples, which would not be destroyed.

"Malta was the ideal place, although it was different in those days. It was still well-forested with ficus trees. There were only a few goatsherds living here.

"We chose one of the highest spots, to keep it safe from any floods. This is why we survived the Great Flood which cut Malta off from the mainland."

"But who do you believe in," she asked.

"The one true God," he replied, without hesitation.

Josephine paused, taking in all this man was telling her and trying to relate it to what she already knew about that period of history. One question sprung to mind: "But why did you leave here?"

The man looked at her and smiled slightly.

"We didn't. We stayed in Malta. We are your ancestors."

Josephine looked at the man's foreign yet familiar face. Perhaps this ancestry explained the Maltese talent for business and music. But she did not have much more time to wonder.

The man stood up to leave. They shook hands politely.

"Whenever you need help," he told her, "come and pray here."

And he walked away.

Was he a messenger from the past? It was not the first time that Josephine had sensed an inexplicable atmosphere at the site. Long before she had met this strange man, Josephine remembered some soldiers who used to be billeted near Hagar Qim confiding that they used to hear singing there, decades before. Perhaps this ancient people still worshipped there, in the dead of night.

In any case, she did call her friend Mr Mintoff.

"Yes," he recalled, when I spoke to him. "She told me that she had met someone from Israel who asked for the temple to be kept sacred. She did not say that he was a ghost at the time," he added, with a little laugh. "I don't believe in these things."

There were many protests about the damage to Hagar Qim by the ballets and TV shows and they were eventually stopped. Was it because of the message passed on to the prime minister?

Dom Mintoff would not say, adding that there were many reasons behind the decision to halt performances.

But he still remembers Josephine's plea on behalf of the Jew...

*****

Most archaeologists date Hagar Qim to around 5,000 years ago, around the time of the legend of the great flood which filled the Mediterranean basin.

Around 3,000 BC, the flood - possibly Noah's in the Bible - was supposed to have buried the Mediterranean basin under several hundred feet of sea-water.

But other theories exist about Hagar Qim. In his

book "Malta's Predeluvian Culture," Joseph S. Ellul explains that he is a descendant of a farmer who worked the lands which virtually covered Hagar Qim at the time of their first excavation in the 19th century. His father was put in charge of the excavation of the temple by Sir Temi Zammit.

Joseph S. Ellul disagrees with Sir Temi's dating of the temples, however. He is convinced that the temples are pre-deluvian, and gives as proof erosion data, corroborated by a University of London professor of archaeology who visited the site in the 1950s.

This, he claims, would date the earliest construction on the site to 10,000BC, making the temple complex one of the oldest in the Mediterranean.

There are other many aspects of the Jew's story which do not tally with known facts. The temple, was, both in shape and artefacts, linked to the fertility goddess. There was certainly no evidence of the Jewish faith.

CHAPTER EIGHT

Some unexplained phenomena are not about the spirits or ghosts at all, but about people who are psychic. Some are about people who can see into the future. Premonitions may be about the law of averages, mere coincidences. On the other hand....

Life - Saving Vision

In the 1970s, serviceman Bob Smith was based at the Plymouth Rescue Co-ordination Centre (SRCC) when a clairvoyant phoned...

The young sailor's departure from the south coast of England was quite an event, drawing a crowd of well-wishers and the curious. He was setting off on a single-handed trip on a yacht across the Channel, but within a few hours, the trip had turned to disaster. He had to abandon ship, drifting in an orange life-raft.

The SRCC mounted a full-scale search, helped by their French counterparts. A whole fleet of helicopters, fixed-wing aircraft and seacraft combed the area for days, as anxious relatives waited desperately for news. But as the days passed, one after the other, the grim reality started to sink in. The chances of survival in the Channel in a liferaft, after that length of time, were slim. The search, in accordance with SRCC guidelines, was called off. The relatives were inconsolable, unable to accept that there was no more hope.

Bob was on duty one night towards the end of that week. After the constant tension of the previous week, things had slowed down to a boring, monotonous routine again. Bob was in the control room, trying to keep awake with a mixture of cigarettes and coffee. He was almost relieved when the phone rang at around three in the morning. "Excitement at last," he muttered wryly to himself.

But the male voice at the other end of the line was quite business-like. "You don't know me, my name is Brown. I'm a clairvoyant," he said.

Bob groaned inwardly. Not another nutter. He

took another sip of the now cold coffee and grimaced. But the man went on: "I've seen a vision." The man described seeing a young man in an orange boat.

Bob groaned even more, now convinced that the man was just wasting his time. Many people who watch intense media coverage in cases like this feel terribly helpless. Some of them want to feel that they are doing their bit, and call the authorities with useless or even imagined information. But Bob went through the routine anyway.

"I see, sir. And where exactly was the boat?" he asked, fully expecting the man to say: "In the sea."

So imagine his surprise when Brown gave him the exact co-ordinates: latitude, longitude, even the minutes.

By now, Bob was definitely interested, although his natural scepticism still made him reluctant to pay too much attention to what Brown was saying. He took down the details, thanked Brown with what he describes as his "best PR manner" and hung up.

At first, he did not react. He lit another cigarette and carried on reading the evening paper. But then curiosity got the better of him and he pulled out the Channel charts. At first glance, the co-ordinates certainly seemed logical. He pictured Brown tormented by this image through the night, eventually feeling that he had to do something about it and phoning the SRCC.

Bob made up his mind, pulling out tide-tables, meteorological charts for that week, checking winds, currents, cross-checking them with the areas which had already been searched...

His cigarette burned out, forgotten, in the ash tray. It was feasible, it was just feasible...

Bob spent the rest of the night working out a probability chart, thinking about Brown and the hope that he had just re-kindled, the faint glimmer of hope that the young man might just still be found, perhaps alive.

By the time the Wing Commander came in at around nine in the morning, Bob was barely able to stop himself from blurting out his discovery. He kept telling himself that he was still unconvinced by the clairvoyant, but at the back of his mind nagged the vital question: what if...?

Bob told the Wing Commander about the strange phone call, trying to sound tongue-in-cheek to protect himself from ridicule, but his experienced superior realised that the information had been accurate enough to merit at least some attention

"What aircraft have we got in the area today?" he asked.

The centre's staff snapped into action. They found that a French maritime patrol aircraft was scheduled to be near the area later that day. They requested that its route be slightly altered towards the east. The tension at SRCC grew. There was one thought on everyone's mind: even if the lad was found, would it be too late?

The French pilot took off, guided by the probability chart that Bob had worked on at the time when he still thought that Brown was just a 'nutter'. Adjustments were made for the wind, tide and current changes since the early morning phone call. The radar screens hummed quietly, the only sound disturbing the intense concentration at the SRCC.

And then the radio came to life. The French pilot had spotted him. The orange liferaft was still bobbing up and down in the swell. The young man was still alive inside it, waving weakly at the aircraft. A cheer went up on both sides of the Channel.

The French aircraft dispatched a ship to the area, and within an hour, he was safe on board, being warmed up. The news soon spread, with relatives reluctant to believe that there was a happy ending after the disappointments of the previous week.

The young man had spent over a week exposed to the elements, surviving only on the food and water in the emergency kit, but he was alive.

After this incident, clairvoyants were used several times in search and rescue operations, not just at sea, but also in suspected homicide cases.

Fear of Flying

Vince's work as a diplomat meant that he had to travel very often. He was quite used to the routine of airports, tickets, baggage. And anyway, this trip was one he was looking forward to.

He was on his way to Geneva, then his base, to pick up some things for a sojourn in Paris, filling in for a sick colleague.

He was travelling via Rome and by the time he had downed a few drinks with a couple of friends at the airport, and deciphered the incomprehensible announcement over the public address system, he was late for his flight.

As he strolled down the aircraft aisle, he was aware of all the eyes on him, probably thinking: "Oh, he's the one we've all been waiting for."

And wouldn't you know it? His seat was the centre one in the row. The woman sitting in the aisle seat had to get up to let him in.

He did try to nod politely to her once he had sat

down, but she just ignored him and carried on reading her book.

He turned to the other woman sitting by him and felt a little more optimistic. She was quite a stunner, wearing a blue, long-sleeved dress and matching hat.

Perhaps in her mid-40s, she was wearing dark sunglasses, but they only made her seem more alluring. She was quite something, and if the whiff of expensive perfume was anything to go by, quite well off too. He discreetly tried to catch a glimpse of her left hand.

He found he was quite looking forward to the hour-long flight.

It turned out that Eileen was a history of art teacher, and it was her first time overseas. She had never flown before this trip and was absolutely terrified, so perhaps that was why she turned to Vince, starting up a conversation to break the tension she was feeling.

He found out that she was on her way to Nairobi, to attend a conference on women's issues. She chatted on, explaining how she had gone into the US information agency and been given this assignment. She was full of enthusiasm about her big adventure. She had already stopped in Rome to meet the FAO, and was on her way to Geneva to meet the WHO representatives, before going on to Nairobi.

As the flight settled into its normal routine, she seemed to relax and the conversation turned to superstitions.

"I went to a fortune-teller," she explained.

"It was at the circus, just fun, you know," she trailed off.

Vince pressed her a bit. She looked at him and

hesitated before answering him.

"The fortune-teller forecast three misfortunes."

Vince was quite surprised at the fear in her voice. Surely these circus fortune-tellers were just a gimmick? And if not, surely a fortune-teller who did see something lurking in the future, would not actually tell the person?

"I ignored it at first," she added.

"But two bad things have already happened."

With a slight tremor in her voice, she explained that her maid had fallen off a ladder while cleaning her apartment and smashed a priceless collection of Japanese miniatures. Soon after, her neighbour had borrowed her new car and smashed it into a tree. He had not been hurt in the accident, but the insurance had refused to pay up as the neighbour was not covered by the policy.

"And now I am waiting for the third. I shudder to think what it might be."

By the way she looked out of the window, her hand clutching the seat arm between them, Vince was pretty sure that she thought the plane trip would be the next misfortune.

In spite of himself, Vince shuddered. He did his best to reassure her, after all no one had been hurt and it could all have been coincidence. Surely she had no reason to suspect that the third misfortune would be so tragic?

All too quickly, the captain informed them that they were to land in Geneva. Eileen turned to Vince and shyly asked whether he would mind holding her hand till they touched down.

She took off her sunglasses as she spoke, and a pair of deep green eyes looked at Vince, full of apprehension.

Vince most certainly did not mind.

He could feel her fingers tightening on his arm as the runway unfolded beneath the aircraft. As the wheels bumped gently onto the tarmac, Eileen smiled at him and said: "Seems we beat the Grim Reaper".

He laughed nervously.

As the rest of the passengers leapt up to retrieve their baggage, elbows and bags jabbed at them. It was time to leave. They exchanged names and addresses and shook hands, somewhat formally and self-consciously.

They parted.

Vince soon settled down into his Paris office, and in the whirl of activity trying to catch up, he did not have much time to think about his travelling companion until a few days later.

He opened the *International Herald Tribune* and came across a story about a woman who had been murdered in Africa. The woman, who was on an assignment for the USIA, was in Nairobi for a conference.

On her first day there, she had gone out to dinner with some other delegates. They had been held up at gunpoint by a young thief. They all handed over their wallets but it seems that he was jittery and the gun went off, killing the woman.

He could not bear to look at the photo of Eileen's smiling face looking up from the page.

Had the fortune teller's third misfortune really struck?

Receiving Signals

One of the strangest things about ghosts and

apparitions is the fact that some people can see them but not others. It may be very reassuring for those who can't, of course, but this is little consolation to those who can.

Linda fell definitely into the "seeing and believing" group. All through her life, she seemed to pick up signals or sensations that others were totally – blissfully – unaware of.

It seemed that she was able to pick up echoes of traumatic events that had happened on a site, usually horrific deaths. One such case happened in the late 1970s, when she went to stay with an old friend who lived in Pennsylvania. The friend fussed about getting her room ready and realised that she did not have enough pillows.

"I can borrow some from my mother's house. I have a key," the friend explained.

They set off to the nearby house but as soon as they approached the front door, Linda recoiled in horror.

"Don't put the key in the lock," she shuddered. "I don't like it here. Forget about the pillow."

And to her friend's surprise, she grabbed her arm and pulled her away, refusing to go in. But the friend laughed her off, having been in the house regularly without incident. Linda waited by the door while her friend popped into the empty house, but she was not at all surprised to see someone in the upstairs window, watching them as they returned to her friend's car.

She later found out that a former Air Force pilot had died in the house but there was no explanation for why she was the only one to feel or see his presence.

That was not the only case. While she was living

in the Netherlands several years later, she went to stay with a friend in his fairly modern home. When she went upstairs, she felt horribly cold, all her senses suddenly alert. She shook herself. It was a new house, with no history yet, nothing that would account for the feeling of evil. And yet as she stood in the room, she was irresistibly drawn to one of the walls. She slowly reached out her hand and placed it flat on the wall.

She drew it away in shock. The wall was freezing cold.

Startled, she almost ran out of the room, and bumped straight into the arms of her friend, who almost seemed to be waiting for her in the corridor.

"Did you see him?" he asked, his voice devoid of any emotion. "Don't worry. You're not the only one. Many others have seen a man in that room."

Linda's impression of evil had been well-founded. Her friend admitted that the house had been built over the site of an old farmhouse that had been demolished as no-one would live in it. The man who lived there had slaughtered his family and then killed himself.

But all the incidents pale beside the experiences she went through in her own house.

Linda moved to the Netherlands in 1973, and lived with her husband and two children in a pretty village near the border with Germany and Belgium.

It was a quaint house, with a fireplace in every room and a rambling garden. It had a huge, sombre attic, with a wooden floor that was so warped and buckled that furniture had to be tied to the wall to stop it from sliding away.

It was really no surprise that the house would settle imperceptibly, creaking and cracking its ancient, wooden joints.

But they were the sort of noises you would hear in any large, old house. They certainly did not explain why Linda found it so hard to find babysitters. None of the girls recommended to her would accept to stay in the house any later than 10 o'clock. But they would refuse to say why, sheepishly blaming it on homework or such, even though she knew that they often babysat for her neighbours through the night.

Eventually, one admitted that the house had a reputation for "strange noises".

And she began to wonder. She had never felt quite alone in the house, and would often find herself standing at her bedroom door, staring with morbid fascination at the closed attic door. She would shake herself, trying to convince herself that there was no one on the other side of it.

But one night, she wondered whether her instinct was right. Maybe there was someone there.

She woke up, cold and suddenly wide awake. There was a shadow in her doorway.

She fumbled in the dark for her glasses and quickly put them on.

A young woman, aged in her late 20s, was floating in the doorway, filling the space in a nebulous cloud, a diaphanous veil drifting in the air around her.

Blinking furiously, Linda shook her sleeping husband. He snored once and turned over, pulling the blankets tighter around him. She pushed and shook him, but he remained resolutely asleep.

The figure drifted away. She looked first at the empty doorway and then at her sleeping husband. She must have dreamt it. She must have.

Linda said nothing about her strange sighting, writing it off to herself as a dream, provoked by her babysitter's talk of noises. But it was not that easy to explain away the next two times she saw the strange, translucent character hovering in the corridor outside her bedroom. Those times, she had been wide awake.

She was evidently not alone in her sensitivity. A girlfriend once came to her house for a chat and walked straight out again, unable to explain why she felt stifled, unable to breathe.

Her teenaged brother came to stay with them and offered to babysit. When Linda and her husband came back, she found all the lights of the house switched on. He had gone to sleep in one of the kid's rooms, fully clothed.

"The noises," he shrugged.

One year, she visited her family in Malta and roped a male friend into watering their plants while she was away. She was really quite surprised when she returned a few weeks later and found that all the plants were dead. He was a reliable sort of person and she preferred to give him the benefit of the doubt.

But even she was not prepared for his story.

"Man, I don't know what you have in your house," he said, trying hard to sound blasé about it. "But it sure doesn't like me." He explained that as he was pottering around downstairs, he heard footsteps going up into the attic. Not one to allow his imagination to run away with him, he headed upstairs. But when he flung open the door, all he could see were the indistinct shapes of furniture, their edges blurred under dustsheets. The attic was utterly silent, nothing moved. He turned back, shaking his head and reprimanding himself for allowing his imagination to get the better of him. But as soon as he picked up the watering can, he heard the footsteps again. And then again.

Until then, he managed to shrug off the strange sensation. But the third time proved too much even for him. He heard the attic door open and close and then the footsteps slowly but surely could be heard coming down the stairs.

"I'm sorry," he shrugged. "But that's when I said *'adios'* and legged it out of there."

But strangely enough, whatever the apparition was did not have the same effect on Linda. She actually felt filled by a tremendous feeling of well-being whenever she saw the image or heard any strange noises. Perhaps whatever it was only reacted against outsiders.

She tried hard to find an explanation for the apparition, but the house did not seem to have any history of trauma. There was only one possible explanation that nagged at the back of her mind.

The village had been one of the innocent war casualties and had suffered at the hands of bombers bound for towns on the German border. Many of the two-storey houses had been hit and because of the shortage of wood, parts of the older houses had been cannibalised to build their replacements or to repair them. Perhaps the ghost had been brought to the house in the remnants of another?

And there the story would have ended. Linda would probably have never said anything to me about the story, after all these years. But some 10 years later, once they had moved out of the house, her husband jokingly brought up the subject of the strange noises.

"You know, I think maybe there was a ghost," he said tentatively. "I think I may have seen it. One night I woke up suddenly and saw the shape of a woman in the doorway to our bedroom.

"It didn't seem at all intimidating and I tried to wake you, but you just wouldn't wake up. You must have been really deeply asleep, because I really shook you," he continued.

"I guess I was probably just dreaming."

The Burden Of Knowledge

The ability to communicate with ghosts is a terrible responsibility

Terence sits quite calmly in his chair, not even noticing the ash that falls silently to the floor from his cigarette. To look at him, you would think that he is talking about something he saw on television. There is no sign of agitation, no hint of fear, no manic glint in his eyes.

But Terence is no ordinary person. As he recounted his tales, one after the other in a relentless stream of incredible phenomena, I could feel a tingle of fear run along my spine. I wriggled in my seat, as though myself afraid of the power he could wield.

Of all the people I have spoken to for this series, he had the most bizarre tales of all.

Because Terence has inherited a very special talent from his maternal grandmother: the ability to communicate with ghosts. This must conjure up images of a medium and seances, but Terence is far from that. Like his grandmother before him, he is able to pick up the "vibrations" in houses, and would know, just know, that there was 'something' there. His mother did not have the same sensitivity, but she accepted her son's power, as she had had to accept her own mother's.

As a child of six, he often accompanied his mother and grandmother while they looked at houses to buy, and he and his gran would exchange knowing glances, "Something not quite right here..."

And then his grandfather died and the young Terence often went to sleep at his grandmother's house, which was more convenient for school. After supper, he would shut the *antiporta* and go up to bed. Seemingly moments later, he would hear a lot of noise and would go down to find the door open again.

His gran always went to hear mass at five o'clock and he would be awakened, not just once but regularly, by someone opening and shutting the *persjani* on the bedroom windows. Then the tap would open in the bathroom next door and he would have to go and turn it off before the bath filled.

These manifestations have already been described to me by other people in other cases. What set Terence's story apart was the fact that he could 'see' the ghost, not in any sense that we would understand or recognise, but rather telepathically. The ghost was a little Turkish boy, with a dark complexion. He did not always appear in the same guise, but more often than not, he – strangely enough – had a mass of golden curls.

The 'boy' would roam restlessly around the house, searching for who knows what. But Terence knew that he was searching for something.

Only once did the 'boy' communicate with Terence. He was once crossing the corridor and noticed that the normally closed cellar door was open. The boy stood in the doorway, beckoning to him.

Many years later his aunt admitted that she had also seen the ghost of a Turkish boy when she had slept in the house. She had been woken up by the sound of her child crying and had found the 'boy' standing in between her bed and the cot rocking the child gently back to sleep.

The house in Sliema has now been demolished. But the ghost is still there, still searching for something or somewhere. Whenever Terence goes by, he can sense his presence, and knows that if he tried to, he would be able to communicate with him. But he never has. "What would be the point? It is a tremendous responsibility. Once they tell you their problem, you feel morally bound to try to help," Terence explained.

The story is made even more intriguing by the fact that a Turk has been seen in neighbouring flats. Terence has also heard that another couple in the same block of flats were disturbed one night by someone knocking at the door. The woman answered to find a little Turkish boy standing there, but by the time she turned to call her husband, he had disappeared.

Who could the boy have been? According to rumours, the house was once used as a billet by soldiers and a young boy had once disappeared there. Is there some secret connected to the house? The only person who could find out is Terence, and he either does not want to find out, or does not want to say.

This is by no means Terence's only story. About 12 years ago, he went to visit some friends in Paris. On their way to dinner, they took a short cut through an alley, one of those typical Parisian tenement buildings, with a courtyard in the centre. As soon as he stepped out of the relative darkness of the alley into the courtyard, Terence knew that there was someone there. He could 'see' a young girl, wearing a flowing dress, cut demurely under her chest, carrying a hoop. The girl called out to him, insisting that she was innocent.

"It was not my fault," she said. "Tell them that it was not my fault." Terence's friends stopped and looked at him in amazement. They could not see or hear anything, and were only aware that their friend was staring at an empty wall. "Terence?" his friend said. The ghost of the girl was a bit taken aback by the intrusion. She backed off saying: "You will pass this way again one day, and then I will tell you the story."

Terence went on to have dinner with his friends. He told them what he had seen, knowing that he would not be in Paris long enough to find out what the young girl had been talking about. His friends listened politely, not quite sure what to make of this remarkable story. But they must have been impressed enough to make some enquiries. They found from local folklore that over a century before, a drunken soldier had forced his way into one of the apartments upstairs and had tried to rape a 13-year-old girl. The girl was terrified and ran from his unwelcome embraces, only to fall to her death on the courtyard below.

And now it seems, she still waits, hoping to protest her innocence to anyone who can hear her impassioned plea.

****

Terence took a deep drag from his cigarette and breathed deeply before he felt ready to tell me more about his harrowing experiences. He eventually leaned forward in his chair, and his voice dropped to an emotional whisper.

It was easy to understand why when he started his story.

Some 10 years ago, he had been studying in Amsterdam. He loved the city, it was full of life, and the year passed all too quickly. But one night still haunts him.

He was staying in a guest-house, in small but comfortable rooms. One night, at around five, he woke up, possessed by a strange sensation. The room was pitch-black, but as soon as he sat up, he was aware of a person towering over him. The man was tall, black and scruffily dressed. But there was something more. An aura of evil emanated from him like tendrils trying to worm their way into Terence's soul.

Terence found that the man's thoughts were whispering in his mind. "Do you want money? Do you want power?" The whispers became more and more insistent, louder and louder.

Terence tried to close his mind off to the preying thoughts but the man was more powerful, more desperate. "All could be yours if you just let me use your body." Terence could feel himself gagging, the panic rising. He suddenly remembered that he had a rosary bead somewhere, one his mother had surreptitiously packed when he left Malta. But where was it? He jumped out of bed and crossed the room, not even aware that he was bumping into furniture. "Imagine how famous you could become... You seem to be an ambitious man, wouldn't you like to be the best?" The cloying voice seemed to fight its way into his mind and he was unable to resist,

He frantically opened drawers and cupboards, pulling out clothes and underwear until his probing fingers found the cold, plastic beads. As soon as he recited the first Hail Mary, he felt an overwhelming release. He felt control over his mind, could close the mental doors one by one to keep the man's threats and promises out. The man faded away and soon Terence was left standing alone in the darkened room, covered in a cold sweat and shivering with fear.

He could not get back to sleep and after hours of pacing up and down, trying to shake off the palpable feeling of evil which lingered in the room, he decided to get out of the house. Outside, he ran into a friend, a nurse who worked in the casualty department of a nearby hospital. She was just coming back from her night-shift and was too tired to notice Terence's ashen face. "There was a terrible accident last night," she prattled on. "This man was already almost dead when they brought him in, it was too late. We couldn't really do anything for him."

Terence was suddenly overwhelmed by the memory of that echoing voice: "Just give me your body..."

"Yes," he said to the nurse. "I know. He was a tall negro, wasn't he?"

She looked at him, taken aback. "How on earth did you know?"

Even if he could have found the courage to speak, Terence could never have explained.

****

When Terence's paternal grandmother died, she left a huge, rambling house in Attard. Many of her relatives at first thought of moving in there, but it was eventually decided to sell the house. Terence and his dad, Edward, went there for one last look. Terence said nothing as they walked around, but as soon as they got back into the car, Terence turned to his dad: "It's a good thing that you have decided to sell the house because there is a ghost." His dad looked at him, somewhat impatiently. "Don't be silly, I didn't see anything." Terence decided to keep quiet. He was in no doubt whatsoever but realised it was useless trying to persuade his sceptical father.

As they walked across the hall, there was a man watching them from the top of the sweeping staircase. He was stockily built and was wearing only a flannel vest and a pair of grubby shorts. The man had just looked down and did not say anything and yet the vibes that Terence picked up were prickly and uncomfortable.

Eventually an Englishman decided to buy the property, and Terence's father warned him not to say anything about the ghost in case they lost the sale. When they eventually met to sign the *konvenju*, they were both surprised when the Englishman looked Edward squarely in the eye, and said: "Why didn't you tell me that the house is haunted?"

Edward hesitated for a moment, not quite sure what to say. Eventually he blurted out a "No, it isn't. I don't believe in that sort of thing".

But the Englishman smiled slowly and turned to Terence. "You may not have known but your son did... Don't worry," he continued. "I'm taking the house because I get on quite well with the ghost. But he didn't like your son." It seems Terence had met a kindred spirit, someone else who could communicate with ghosts.

The man bought the house although it has since been re-sold. It is still lived in.

****

These stories are all just the tip of the iceberg. Terence's life is a sequence of stories, starting from when he was a child. Some of the experiences were positive, others not.

His maternal grandmother died when he was in his 20s, and for a long time after, he would be aware of her coming into the room. She would cross to a chair at the far end of the room and watch the family. She always brought with her an aura of peace and tranquility.

But Holland was a bad phase for him. His psychic powers seemed to be heightened and he once found himself talking in a different voice – and a different language which he thinks was Egyptian. He thinks that it may be evidence of a previous life, but it is a subject he seemed to shy away from.

To most other people, his powers are totally invisible, but other psychics seem to be able to recognise each other. Once when he was in his 20s, he was down at Exiles beach when a total stranger walked over to him and took him aside. "We need a medium..." the man said. Terence pulled back, asking: "Why me?" The man only looked at him and said: "You know why."

Terence is very aware of the power he possesses and it is truly tempting to use it sometimes. Many of his close friends know about his experiences and he has been asked a number of times to go to their houses to check out possible ghosts. But he does not see himself as some romanticised ghost-buster. Far from it. He is a quiet man, now in his mid-forties, who lives on his own, totally dedicated to his work. He has turned down all requests to "make contact" with ghosts.

But in spite of his determination to lead as normal a life as possible in the circumstances, sometimes, against his will, contact is made. Six months ago, he was woken up by someone brushing his foot and then his hand. He knows that it was the soul of someone dying, a spirit changing state from life to after-life.

Terence had worked his way through a pack of cigarettes by the time he had told me his story. He got up to leave but I sat there glued to the chair, mesmerised. It cannot be easy bearing the burden of all those trapped souls, all those spirits trying to find someone to release them. He gave a tired shrug before he went out.

CHAPTER NINE

This story simply does not fit into any category at all. Josephine Burns Debono was in her late 80s when I spoke to her. She wanted her story to be told. The story may sound incredible yet, on checking, I found that all the details, dates and places fitted in with documented facts.

Edward Agius was no ordinary man. Although he was not an official diplomat, he played an important role in his unofficial capacity, shuttling between England and the continent at the turn of the century. He spoke an impressive 19 languages.

Josephine says it was he who apparently coined the phrase *"entente cordiale"* over a brandy with the French president of the time. She is clearly proud of her grandfather but the story she told would give him an even more important role in history - that of helping to convert the British king, Edward VII to Roman Catholicism.

Josephine's story is regarded with understandable scepticism, even by her own family, but she was still remarkably sprightly for her age and her memory had certainly not been affected by time. This is the story she told me.

Before one of Edward Agius' frequent trips to France in the 1860s, the weather had been too rough to permit the sea passage across the British Channel and he found shelter for the night at a quiet inn in Dover. There was only one other person in the restaurant at the time, a young man. Picking up his cognac, he wandered over and asked whether the man would mind if they shared what was left of the evening together.

The man said his name was Baron Renfrew. Edward Agius raised his eyebrow, although only slightly. Renfrew was the name used by the Prince of Wales when he wanted to travel incognito, Albert Edward, who would eventually become Edward VII. He had just got engaged to Princess Alexandra and had been banished to Paris by his mother, Queen Victoria. He said it was to learn French, but he made it clear that he was well aware that his mother wanted him out of her sight.

The two men immediately hit it off and the Prince spent some time with him in Paris.

A year later, Prince Albert married Princess Alexandra, but he never really gave up his bachelor life, having one affair after another, many of them well publicised.

Once on the throne, one of the king's frequent trips overseas took him to Italy. One of the women in the party suggested that they dine at a Dominican monastery near Florence, which had been recommended for its excellent food. The king was captivated by the way of life and the calm, serene atmosphere. The seed was sown.

The king wanted to know more about Roman Catholicism and by April, 1903, it had become an obsession.

By then, Edward Agius had been made an agent of the Pope. He suggested that the king speak to the Pope about his wish to convert. The king was going to Italy and did in fact see Pope Leo XIII although there is no official record of what they discussed in private.

Josephine said that the Pope would not hear of the conversion. He advised the king that as the head of the church of England, converting to Roman Catholicism would be impossible, unthinkable. He told him gravely that it was something he could only contemplate on his death bed, when it would be a private decision between him and His Maker.

The words were to make a deep impact on the king. He confided in his friend Edward and the two of them arranged for a Maltese Dominican priest, Innocenzo Apap to go to Edward's house at Belsize Grove in Hampstead, every Monday afternoon.

The king went there in an unmarked carriage and had tea with the family, including the toddler grandchild Josephine, who had lived with Edward since her father had died when she was just a year old. Josephine still clearly recalls being bounced on the king's knee and eating strawberry jam and butter sandwiches.

After tea, the king retired to the library with the Dominican priest where they discussed the teachings of the church.

The clandestine Monday meetings continued for many years but then in 1910, the king went to Paris and Biarritz and caught a bad cold, which he could not shake off. By the time he returned to England, it had become bronchitis and he had a series of heart attacks. Queen Alexandra knew that the situation was serious.

It had all been carefully arranged. She sent a note to Edward Agius, who called for Fr Apap. Dressed in plain clothes, they were taken to the Palace where they waited. They were eventually shown into the king's room by a back entrance and there King Edward VII was converted to Roman Catholicism. It was as he wished it to be, just between him and his conscience. Edward Agius and Fr Apap respected his wish for secrecy.

Two months later, Josephine was taken upstairs by her nanny Clara Porter. They were on their way to pray at the little chapel they had there and found Josephine's aunt, Daisy, there, arranging red roses on the altar.

And there, sitting on the chair was the ghost of the king, dressed in a bright green velvet coat.

"Oh, the king," Clara cried out, totally bewildered. Josephine was totally unself-conscious. She ran to take her accustomed place on his lap.

"Where is your father?" the king asked.

Business, she replied. Her aunt Daisy added, hesitantly: "My brother is in the city."

"Will you tell him that I am in heaven where they are treating me well," he said. "Tell him that all our efforts were worth while."

He patted Josephine on the head and got up. He walked away and simply disappeared, leaving Clara and Daisy in tears.

Josephine claimed that apart from a few family members who knew of the conversion, Edward Agius and Innocenzo Apap took the story with them to their graves, but she decided that the story should be told.

A year before, she did write and tell the story to Cardinal Hume, but there is nothing in writing to substantiate her story and the cardinal apparently felt he could take it no further.

Rumours of the king's obsession with Roman Catholicism are documented, and Fr Apap was well known for his work in establishing contact with different religions in London at the time. Other dates and details also tally with biographies of the king.